Ocean's Pearl

Enjoy!

چنین بود! ؟

وهابیون

Ocean's Pearl

Rowan Todd

Published by Tablo

For Mia,

You were so brave for such a long time,

I will never forget you.

Chapter 1

The ocean and pearls. Two natural phenomena.

Pearls are made when bacteria is trapped inside a shell. An immune response locks this bacteria inside. Over the coming years a pearl is formed. The ocean keeps the treasure safe and cradles it like a mother cradling her newborn child.

Pearls and the ocean. Two natural phenomena.

I suppose our names are quite fitting then. A pair of identical twins. There's me Ocean (the oldest by ten minutes) and then there's Pearl. We are an exact mirror image of each other. I write with my left hand, she writes with her right. I have a mole on my right cheek, she has one on her left. I have a birthmark on my left thigh, she has one on her right. Exact mirror images.

I sit on my bed, on the right side of the room which Pearl and I share. Our house is big enough to have a room each but we can't bear the thought of sleeping in different places and not being able to talk. There's the relaxed, light, airy feeling which is always in the air by this point in the summer holidays. No school work for another ten days at least. Heaven. I scroll down my Instagram feed on my iPhone.

Pearl starts laughing from her bed on the left hand side of the room. She's probably laughing at some video that Madeline sent to her. She keeps laughing for like ten minutes. I look up from my phone at my twin. It's difficult not to love her. Her laugh is something out of this world and whenever she laughs you want to laugh with her.

"And breathe," I say, trying not to crack up as I make chill-the-hell-out motions with both my arms. However my attempt doesn't work and before long I'm giggling along with her. That's how infectious my sister's laugh is.

"We'd probs best start packing," says Pearl, getting up from her bed. I nod; yes, packing for our annual trip to the Harbour Hotel in Littlehampton on the Sussex coast. We've waited all summer holiday for this, with mum working full tilt at the hospital, whilst hearing from our friends about all their amazing trips to here, there and everywhere. Finally it's our turn.

We find our matching suitcases in the cupboard under the stairs and roll them out. We each pack almost the exact same things. Two t-shirts, two pairs of shorts, an evening dress (just in case), jeans, hoody, PJs and rain coats (you can never be quite sure what the weather will be like in the British summer time). Pearl also packs Bumble, her beloved teddy bear.

"You're so babyish," I tease.

Now we both flop down onto our beds. The summer holidays make me so chilled! It's a different pace from term time and I was *so* ready for the break after the endless drone of teachers saying

'The next two years are the most important school years so far'

'Remember, starting work on your GCSE's over the summer will help you get good grades.'

'Blah, blah…'

Naturally I haven't so much as opened a book and it's nearly term time again!

I look around our baby pink coloured room. Every other patch of wall is covered either with my art work, or framed poems written by Pearl. Mum's good like that. Ever since I can remember she's always displayed our creative work in pride of place. She's always telling us to believe in ourselves.

"Just think," says Pearl, "This time tomorrow we'll be in the pool or playing cards or whatever. It'll be the best."

I nod in agreement. We always have a blast in Littlehampton, even when Mum and Dad are arguing, which is happening more and more. I can't imagine having fights every day with Pearl, in fact I think I can count on one hand the amount of arguments we've ever had.

We hear the ice cream van down on the street below. It's been doing a roaring trade this summer with the warm weather we've had.

"Let's go get ice cream," I say, jumping up from my bed.

"Yay!" squeals Pearl like a five year old.

We take some two pound coins from our money box and run down the street. There's already a big queue starting to form.

"This could take some time," I say, rolling my eyes. There's all the usual hullabaloo going on with toddlers dropping their flakes and a young child's lolly melting off the stick. By the time we get to the front of the queue there's no ice creams left.

"Sorry," says the man in the van, "People just get so excited."

I open my mouth and am about to say some choice phrases but I get a nudge from Pearl who I swear can read my mind.

"That's fine, enjoy your day," says Pearl.

"That's half an hour of our life gone. We'll never get it back. I wish there was such a thing as time insurance," I rant as we walk home.

"It could be a lot worse you know, at least we had the money to even think about getting an ice cream."

I nod knowing she's right and wish I could be as kind and sweet as she is.

We knock on our front door and a gentle summer breeze blows our blond hair softly back behind us. Dad answers and we step in.

"What ice cream did you get?" asks Dad, a smile peeping out from his black beard and mustache.

"Nothing" I say.

"They'd completely sold out by the time we'd got to the front of the queue," Pearl adds.

"Oh that's annoying," says Dad sympathetically. "However I'm about to go to the shop to get some grab-and-go breakfast stuff for tomorrow. Do you want to come? We could get a four pack of ice cream for half the price of what you'd pay at the van. "

We nod and walk with Dad the two streets and cross the main road to the local Sainsbury's. We head inside and Pearl picks up a basket. We stroll through the aisles and pick a four pack of fruit lollies and a four pack of breakfast bars for tomorrow. We walk back slowly to our house, licking our cool, fruity treats as we go.

When we arrive there, Pearl and I decide to go to the local swing park for a bit. Dad says this is okay and we stroll down the road. It's a beautiful play park inside a much bigger green area with a hill in the middle. Pearl and I used to roll down that hill and played on it all the time when we were smaller. As could have perhaps been predicted, the playground bit is heaving, but that's okay, we're probably too old to go on the roundabout, well with other people looking anyway! Instead we walk up to the top of the hill. It may just be a mound of earth but to us it's like a monument to our childhood. I take out my phone and put my iTunes on shuffle and we head bang along to *Baby* by Justin Bieber, *Bad Romance* by Lady Gaga and *Timber* by Ke$ha. We laugh and I doodle on a drawing app on my phone while Pearl reads. Ms Williams, our art teacher, says that I have a real talent for art. I've chosen it for one of my GCSE subjects starting in year ten in September and one day I'd love to be able to sell my work.

We walk back to our house and knock on the door.

We hear Mum shouting:

"Well that's fine for you isn't it?"

Then we hear Dad replying in the same tone:

"Oh stop talking crap!"

Knowing that neither of them will hear us over their row we unlock the key from the keysafe and open the door ourselves, tiptoeing back inside and wondering if this latest argument will impact on the rest of our holidays.

Chapter 2

For dinner we use up all the fresh foods in the fridge.

"So what is everyone most looking forward to about our holiday?" asks Pearl, dipping a carrot stick into some hummus.

"I'm looking forward to not having to do any cooking or cleaning for the next week," says Dad.

"And what is that supposed to mean?" Mum interrogates.

"It was a flippant comment," defends Dad.

And just like that a perfectly nice meal has descended into World War Three.

Pearl and I finish eating as soon as possible to avoid getting caught up in the heated exchange. We quickly clear our plates to the side and then head up the stairs into our room. We huddle under our eiderdowns to try and ignore Mum's shouting.

"You think I do no work when I am on the front line of the NHS saving lives? Whereas you've had a failed career!"

It's been like this all summer. Dad at home keeping things going. Mum doing extra consultant shifts at the hospital and neither of them very happy. We both feel smaller than ever when they shout.

"At least I'm vaguely content, unlike you!" Dad screams.

The argument goes on and on.

"You okay?" I ask my twin, as softly as is audible over the din of the kitchen argument.

"Yeah," says Pearl, "Well, I guess not, I mean... Do you think they're gonna split up?"

I'm about to say *Yes, well, duh!* but Pearl's pleading blue eyes make me change my mind.

"No of course not, I think they're just having a bit of a bump in the marital road."

"I think it's a bit more than that," says Pearl sadly.

"Well yes… okay… a pot hole in the road."

Pearl giggles.

"Yeah, like a really big pot hole that jiggles the car around for a little bit, that's all that's going on."

Pearl and I get into our pyjamas and rummage through our suitcases to find our toothbrushes. We clean our teeth and brush our hair in front of the mirror. After this we get into our beds. We listen to Mum and Dad. It's difficult not to listen sometimes. Suddenly there's a loud, angry knocking at the front door. We hear it being opened then the annoyed voice of Sonja, our next door neighbour.

"Do you mind?" she whispers irritably, "Some of us are trying to get young children to sleep which is impossible with your racket. Stop shouting or I will call the police," she warns and then the door slams.

Now there's only silence in our house. We hear Mum's footsteps heading into the bedroom they share and then the sound of Dad getting the sofa bed out downstairs.

"The holiday will be lovely regardless," I say to myself and I guess to Pearl.

"How do you know?" asks Pearl.

"Well obviously I don't know," I say sadly, "but I do know that you and I are gonna have, like, such a good time."

"What will we do?" asks Pearl.

"All the usual," I say. "So when it's hot you and I will go to the beach and we'll swim in the sea and eat ice cream and then we'll go get fish and chips. Oh yeah, and when the seagulls see what we're eating they'll try and dive bomb us."

"What about when the weather is rainy and British-Summer-Timey?" asks Pearl, although she knows the answer.

"We'll play Uno in our room and hysterically laugh when one of us forgets to say *Uno* and has to pick up two extra cards. When we're bored of that we'll get room service from the bar and get crisps, J2Os and sandwiches and eat and drink on our beds while we watch back to back old episodes of Casualty. After we've done that we'll go swimming in the indoor pool and get like seriously competitive."

"<u>You</u> will you mean," Pearl interjects.

"Yes, alright <u>I</u> will. But anyway, we'll swim for like an hour and then we'll get dressed and go get afternoon tea or hot chocolate at the bar."

I can tell that my plans are making Pearl sleepy so I carry on.

"So after we've had hot chocolate we'll go back to our room and do some art, drawing or reading or something. So then we'll go to Mum and Dad's room and we'll go to dinner with them and stuff ourselves on the all-you-can-eat buffet. We'll have like five helpings each and go into a food coma and have to lie down for a while and then…"

But I stop because Pearl is now fast asleep.

Chapter 3

The crunchy combination of mine and Pearl's different alarm ringtones jolts me from sleepiness. Normally I'm the Morning Person, but it's Pearl who immediately sits up and gets straight out of bed.

"Come on Oceay," she says to me, as I groan sleepily from under my thin summer eiderdown, "We need to get dressed!"

I roll back over onto my side.

"Come on Oceay," she says, ripping my eiderdown off my bed.

"Right," I start, "You'll pay for that!" I take my pillow out from under my head, quickly sit up and start hitting Pearl with it. She now grabs her pillow and before long we are engrossed in a full on pillow fight.

We stop once we hear Mum's angry footsteps coming from Mum and Dad's room heading for our door.

"What the hell?" she hisses, "It's half past seven. You've probably woken up the entire street!"

"Well," I reason, "You did say we have to be on the road by eight."

Mum looks livid and walks back out again.

"Morning to you too Mum!" I mutter.

Pearl and I slip on some denim shorts and white flowy tops. Once we are dressed we style our hair into matching plaited buns. Well, I style mine and then do Pearl's as she's never been much good at doing her own hair. We roll our suitcases into the kitchen and feel them glide along the smooth, dark brown floorboards over to the sofa bed, now made sofa again.

Dad is busying himself behind us, hastily organising snacks for the car journey so we won't have to pay a fortune for food when we stop at a service station, even though we all know, despite his efforts, we'll be getting a burger anyway.

"You two alright?" he asks, whilst packing four packets of crisps into a fabric bag.

"Yeah," says Pearl "I'm good."

"That's good," he smiles, showing off his crooked teeth. "What about you Ocean?" he asks while filling up four bottles of water.

"I'm doing... great," I lie. "I can't wait to arrive in Littlehampton!" This bit is true. I do always look forward to our annual seaside trip.

"I can't wait either," says Dad walking over into the sofa area. "It's gonna be so much fun."

"What about you and Mum?" asks Pearl.

Dad opens his mouth and looks like he's about to say something but then Mum enters the room and Dad quickly shuts it again.

"Look at my beautiful girls all grown up. Done their own packing and everything."

Her warm words make me glow. She's clearly making an effort to be the lovely sunny mum I know she can be. She even gives Dad a slight smile.

Truce?

Pearl and I walk into the hallway and crouch down to tie our blue converse trainers. We use the exact same bunny ear's tying method. We simultaneously stand up and head out of our front door. Mum and Dad follow and Dad shuts the door behind him. We walk out onto the street to our car, load our suitcases into the back and get in. Pearl and I are in the back and Mum and Dad in the front, with Mum driving. I open up a breakfast bar and take a large bite, the rich nutty, raisin flavours fill my mouth and I close my eyes to enjoy every chew I take. I finish it and stuff the wrapper in my pocket, making a note to put it in a bin when we stop.

I now plug in my headphones, put my iTunes music on shuffle and let my feet dance along to *Story Of My Life* by One Direction, I shake my shoulders along to *Galway Girl* by Ed Sheeran and mouth along to *Nine To Five* by Dolly Parton. I know I have a strange taste in music, but whatever! After ten minutes I look over to my right and see that Pearl is looking at the window. Knowing she probably has that wide, wistful expression on her face, I decide to remove her from her daydream.

"Pearl?" I call out to her. She whips round.

"Yeah? What?" she asks, trying to sound moody but failing epically.

"I just wanted to chat!" I reply, slightly turning in my seat.

"Okay," Pearl says "What about?"

I ponder for a second then I say, "What we're gonna get from Maccies at the service station."

"Okay," Pearl nods.

"Okay," I say manically. "So I want a Big Mac with fries Happy Meal, a chocolate milkshake and…"

"You'll be sick," giggles Pearl.

"Fine then," I say with mock annoyance, "What are you gonna get?"

"Probably a sandwich or something," she says.

"Uh, you're so boring," I criticise, "Try and think bigger. And when I say bigger I mean bigger portion!"

"Uhm… Okay I'll have two sandwiches and a coke, you know one of those really big ones, the size of your head."

I nod in approval. "Well, it could still do with some work but it's definitely a lot better."

We drive down the M23 and Pearl and I talk excitedly about our plans for our holiday.

"I'm gonna put on so much weight this week," I say while stuffing my face with some salt and vinegar crisps. "I'll be so fat that you'll need a crane to get me into our house."

Pearl giggles, showing off her straight, white teeth which exactly match mine.

Mum and Dad appear to be sitting in icy silence in the front. Maybe I was wrong about the whole truce thing. I wish I understood why they were in this argument in the first place. But I guess it's just one of those things and I'm pretty sure I will never understand it.

We stop after about an hour at a service station but unfortunately there's no McDonalds, so I can't get my dream lunch and I have to settle for a Burger King instead. After I've finished eating, Pearl and I go exploring the service station. We find one of those irritating toy grabbing machines, the ones where you think you're about to win a giant monkey or something and then it drops back down to the toy heap again. We waste fifteen minutes and five quid attempting to rescue a giant panda from the prison that is a toy machine. Dad then buys us a scratch card each and we both win five pounds!

"Holiday savings," says Dad pointing at the smooth plastic notes in our hands.

"What are you going to spend it on?" he asks, looking genuinely interested.

"I'm gonna see when I get there," says Pearl, throwing her right arm out to the side in a *so yeah* kind of way.

Dad nods.

"Nice, and what about you Ocean?"

I'm about to tell him that I'm planning on buying as many sweets and as much junk food as I can, but then I see Mum close by, and to avoid a forty minute lecture on the dangers of sugar and diabetes I smile and nod.

"Same as Pearl," I say.

After Mum and Dad have had a marital, it's decided that Dad will drive the rest of the way.

"You're clearly knackered," he says kindly. "Look, I know you hate driving."

After a few choice words Mum reluctantly agrees and nods.

"FINE!" she growls.

We get back in the car, feeling happy and full up from the food we bought.

"What am I thinking?" I ask, turning to Pearl and blinking at her.

"What?" says Pearl looking confused.

"I want to see if it's true, you know, that twins are telepathic?"

"Okay," says Pearl, looking interested.

"So, what am I thinking?" I ask, blinking again.

"Chocolate," she says, looking happy with herself.

"Yes, right, chocolate," I say with mock frustration, "But what specifically?"

"Uhm… Twix?" she asks.

"No," I say "Curly Wurly,"

"Close though," Pearl protests.

"No," I say, "Completely different."

We play this game back and forth for the next twenty minutes, Pearl smiling all the time. Although we look the exact same, I've always thought there's something prettier about Pearl. Is it her sweet manner? Is it her kind demeanor? Whatever it is, she's destined for far better things than I am.

Suddenly Mum and Dad start arguing again in the front.

"For God's sake Max!" Mum shrieks, "You've just taken a wrong turning!"

"No I haven't," says Dad defensively.

"No, look at the satnav. See? You've gone wrong. Christ's sake, keep your eyes on the road!" she berates. "Watch out!!"

Loud crash followed by another. *What the hell is happening?* I hear Pearl scream. *Am I screaming?* Car launching into space. Heart hard against my chest. Yelling... *Help... Get the car sitting upright again.* Blaze of angry red light. Scorching heat. Hair on fire. Hurts too much to move. Sirens. Searing pain in my flesh. Darkness.

Chapter 4

Floating.

Weightless. Light. Airy.

World below looks strange. What is this place I'm in? It seems… different. Like a dream. Or a dream of a dream. As I look down I wonder: is the world really as kind as I thought or is it really a place of pain and fear? I keep drifting through the sky. Am I flying? I'd be happy to stay here. It would be easy from this distance. Seeing real life drama without it being able to harm me! If I was to stay here, they could all carry on without me.

There are no worries here. None at all.

I think I should start exploring this white wonderland properly when suddenly I feel I'm being pulled downwards.

No! I scream *No! No!*

"No," I ramble, "No."

What's happened to me? One minute I was up wherever that was and now I'm down in wherever this is.

My mouth is a dry desert. My entire body feels like a tonne of bricks, too heavy to lift. Everything screams in pain, my left arm and my left leg crying out the loudest. The agonising sound in my head is so loud I try and screw up my face to stop the noise. But it hurts far too much. I can hear a slow steady *beep, beep, beep* from somewhere around me.

My brain feels active and wants to think and play but my head hurts too much to even contemplate anything. My mind is pretty much empty of everything. Suddenly questions arrive in my brain making my head throb with deep stabs.

Who am I?

Where am I?

What's happened to me?

More and more questions funnel in:

Why am I here?

What's that irritating beep noise?

Why do I feel like my entire body is on fire?

With some time I remember who I am.

I'm Ocean Rodrigo and I've got a twin called Pearl.

But still the questions... the constant questions... increasing and reproducing like fast growing bacteria.

"Stop, stop, stop!" I whisper.

I think I hear footsteps. They seem to be walking towards me.

"Go away," I half shout, thinking the whole thing is an auditory illusion.

A voice replies.

"Well, I can go away if you want."

Okay... Definitely not in my head.

"Who are you then?" I hiss, as I struggle to open my eyes.

"I'm Laura," the voice says.

"Okay," I continue, "And where am I?"

There's a pause.

"Now, I want you to stay calm," Laura says soothingly, the way people do only when they're about to drop a bombshell.

"What is it? What's going on?" I ask anxiously. *I still feel so drowsy.*

"Well... I'm sorry to tell you this but... Ocean... you've been in a bad crash."

My mouth tries to drop open, but the skin feels tight and sore.

"Am I in hospital then?" I ask, my voice increasingly panicked.

"Yes," says Laura hesitantly, "And your injuries are quite extensive."

"Like what?" I ask, anxiety building by the second in my chest.

"Well…" begins Laura, "You have burns all over your body. At times it was very much touch and go."

"Okay…" I start. "How bad are we talking? Do I still look like I did?" I feel panic.

"No," says Laura slowly. She kind of pauses.

"What else?" I'm getting desperate.

"Well… I'm so sorry. Your left leg was trapped under the seat in front of you, the circulation was cut off and they… had to amputate later at the hospital" says the nurse slowly.

"What? You mean like cut off?" I try to shout but my mouth is too dry for much sound to come out.

"I'm so sorry!" says Laura half sobbing.

"Why don't I remember any of this?" I ask.

"You were in and out of consciousness for over a week." says Laura, her voice trembling. "Then you had to have eyelid surgery. You've had bandages on them for the past seven days…"

"My eyes?" I echo.

Suddenly my left arm starts throbbing like mad again.

"Why's my left arm hurting so much?" I ask, feeling certain that I'm about to be shot with another bullet of bad news.

"Your left arm sustained a bad break." Laura says. "They were able to save it though," she gabbles quickly. "It's just still in plaster."

"Why can't I open my eyes?" I ask, trying to blink.

"Your eyes have been taped closed since the surgery to stop the skin grafts being damaged," explains Laura. I hear her taking a seat on a chair I assume is next to my bed.

My mind starts going crazy. It keeps saying things like:

Oh great, they've saved your eyes but they haven't saved your leg.

Will I be able to paint again with a shattered arm?

Suddenly I think of a burning question which is far more important than anything else. I take a deep breath.

"Where's Pearl?" I ask.

Chapter 5

"Pearl?" repeats Laura.

"Yes!" I say. I feel terrified. "My twin."

There's a long pause.

"Tell me what's happened" I say, my throat catching.

"Uhm…" says Laura, "I'm so sorry to tell you this but…" her voice trailing off.

"There were only two survivors in your family."

"Please let the other be Pearl, please let it be Pearl," I whisper, hoping if I say it enough it might become the truth. I take a deep breath.

"So who is the other one?" I ask.

"Your mum." Laura's reply is like a door being slammed.

"What?" I croak. "Pearl's dead? But… but… she can't be dead. She's my twin… she's the same age as me… she's ten minutes younger than me…"

I thought the pain was bad before but now my poor burned skin screams out in pain. The more I process that Mum is the only other survivor, the more I realize the truth.

"Dad?" I ask.

"I'm so sorry," says Laura, putting her hand softly on my right arm.

But he's my Dad. Surely without him being here I cease to exist. I can't imagine a world without Dad's hugs and his amazing chocolate cake. *Pearl, Dad… Dad, Pearl…* the names keep repeating in my head round and round on a loop. I can't bear this. How is this now my life? The pain is extreme. It presses in on my chest like a hundred kilogram dumbbell has been dropped on me. It's excruciating. No matter how many times Laura says *I'm so sorry*, it doesn't go away. In fact the more I think about it the heavier the weight in my chest feels. It twists and turns like a snake, emotional venom releasing into my body. It's five billion times worse than the pain from my physical injuries, and those hurt eleven out of ten. The pain is so agonising, but even yelling doesn't take the edge off. In fact, it multiplies it by a hundred.

I can't believe I've lost her, my friend... my best friend. Nothing will ever heal the hole in me. It'll remain there for the rest of my life - physical scarring and another type of scarring running far deeper.

I'm alive! Why am I alive? Why couldn't I die? Pearl deserved to live! She's a much... was a much better person then I will ever be.

With my eyes taped up I'm not sure how long I scream and wail for: *An hour? A day? Forever?* But at some point I fall back into a troubled sleep. I keep replaying the last time I saw her laugh in the car and I feel for a moment the weight being lifted from me. But then, I hear Laura or one of the other nurses' voice saying, *I'm so sorry,* and then I wake up again, wriggling and screaming. It happens again and again. It never stops. The agony is brutal... and constantly getting worse.

She's never coming back, I think. *I'll never see her beautiful, kind, sweet, loving, friendly, giving, sparkling eyes again. She's gone... disappeared from the face of the earth. What if there's no afterlife? What if she only lives on in my memory?*

At some point I find out that I've missed the funerals. Why did they have to happen so quickly? Now how will I say goodbye? It was just our extended family: Aunt Sophie and Aunty Rose and their children Jack and Holly. That's it... no one else. Apart from Mum, that's the only family I've got left now. I should have a twin … my twin … my best friend… my life-long friend. We had so many plans for the future. We were going to become world famous, Pearl for writing, me for art. Life was meant to be amazing.

And I should have a Dad… my Dad… my not-so-cool role model. Who else will make me laugh with his terrible dancing? Who else will play music all round the house?

Dad, Pearl…Pearl, Dad…

Time drags on and the pain still sits there like a stubborn, heavy rock. Nothing takes the unbearable feeling away, not even the copious amounts of painkillers they're still giving me. The mental anguish is fixed and permanent. I'm not sure if it'll ever go away.

It never will.

I keep going round in circles in my head. I try talking with her telepathically like we did on that fateful day, but there's no response, just my subconscious pretending to be Pearl, which only makes everything hurt a thousand times more.

"Where's my biggest fan?" I ask myself, again and again.

"Who else will laugh at my awful jokes?"

Chapter 6

One morning a few days after I wake up, a doctor called Helena comes in and tells me that the tape over my eyes will be removed today.

"When you were first with us the team were fighting to save you Ocean and it wasn't until a week or so later that you'd stablised enough to have the eyelid grafts. We needed to bandage them to make sure they heal properly. I'm happy for the dressings to come off now."

Save my life? How close was I to not making it then?

"We'll give you some nitrous oxide to ease any pain. So we're planning to do it this morning at some point," she confirms.

Some time later, Helena and Laura come into the room.

"I need you to breathe through this," says Laura, "It's a piece of tubing. Open your mouth." she says, and I oblige.

I start to breathe. At first it feels pointless because everything still hurts. But suddenly I start laughing. It starts as a small giggle. But before long I'm hysterically laughing. My sides ache, but I don't care and just for a second the emotional pain goes from my chest.

"All done!" says Laura, too soon. "You do know that's why they call it laughing gas!"

"Now we're going to turn the lights right down and close all the blinds." says Helena. "It'll be damaging for your eyes if they're overexposed too quickly."

I hear some rustling in the room.

"Okay," says Laura. "Try and open your eyes now."

I start trying to push my eyes open.

"Slowly," says Helena.

I slow it right down, it hurts... It hurts like mad. I think it takes about a minute for me to open my eyes and every millimeter is a struggle. I wish they'd carried on giving me the laughing gas. Once my eyes are open I'm able to blink once, twice. Every time I blink the action feels increasingly easy and familiar. As Helena had said, the room is completely dark.

"Okay," says Laura, after about twenty minutes, "I'm going to turn the light on to its lowest setting. "Okay?" she asks.

"Yes," I say softly.

The light makes me squint, even though the room isn't much lighter than pitch black.

"Right Ocean," says Helena, "We're going to leave it on this setting for a while. Close your eyes just as I leave the room, it's very bright out there."

I do as I'm told, not wanting my eyes to be damaged.

"Once your eyes are functioning at full capacity," say Laura, "We can move you onto the main pediatric burns unit."

"What? No!" I gabble.

The sleep deprivation is bad enough in an isolation room, nurses coming constantly to check your observations and stuff, but main wards are a nightmare. I remember when Dad had a hernia. Mum, Pearl and I went to visit him and he said there was no sleep in hospital. I always thought this was too weird to be true because hospitals should be where you go to rest and recuperate. But it turns out, even in a single room, it's difficult to sleep.

Throughout the day Helena comes in again and again, turning the lights up slightly more each time. By the evening I'm able to squint up at a light at full capacity.

I glance around my room. There's another room connected to my room, I think it's a bathroom, a load of tall machines on wheels and a couple of seats. I inspect the bed. It has sides coming up like a cot. The sides are trapping me in this life which I don't want to live any more.

A life without Pearl seems like a night with no dawn, winter with no Christmas, seasons with no summer. My life now Pearl's not in it feels completely wrong. Like the world has ended. Her life was cut short, gone, just like that but my life goes on. I could live to a hundred - Pearl could have done as well.

I lie awake and I wonder if somewhere, somehow Pearl is doing the same. Does she wonder what it's like for me to live just as much as I wonder what it's like to die.

I then think about Dad, his last conscious moment would have been Mum screaming at him. It's all her fault. If she hadn't screamed at Dad we would have had a lovely holiday at the beach. But instead.... well... instead I'm here. I'm lying in a hospital bed. Will I ever walk again? Will I be confined to a wheelchair for the rest of my life?

I feel a rush of anger towards Mum. It's all Mum's fault. *Why* did she have to shout at Dad? He lost control of the wheel because of her shrieking. My mind continues fretting over these things until I feel myself falling backwards into a troubled night of nightmares, re-living the accident again and again. On repeat.

How will I carry on without Pearl?

I don't know.

I honestly do not know.

Chapter 7

I must have finally drifted off to a deep sleep after that because the next thing I know is someone gently shaking my shoulder the following morning. My mouth is so dry still, and I'm feeling confused.

"There's someone here to see you," says Laura softly.

As I wake up properly I become aware of someone I really recognise at last: Aunt Sophie. She is standing at the end of the bed with her arms stretched wide. Sort of like mum but not. Same height but different eyes and definitely a different style!

"Oh Ocean," she smiles. "I'm so glad to see you. I've been worried to bits about you. This is all so dreadful. Your Dad and Pearl…" she stops in her tracks, suddenly drowned in a wave of sorrow.

"I miss her." I say. "I don't have the words to describe how much I miss her," I say, trying to stop my voice from shaking.

"I understand." says Aunt Sophie, gently placing a hand on my scarred right arm. "And your poor Mum. They don't know how well she's going to recover…" There is a glistening in her eyes.

Aunt Sophie's face reminds me of Mum. Aunt Sophie the lawyer, Mum the medic.

Silence

"I don't know what to say, Ocean. Except we're here for you. Me, Aunty Rose, Jack and Holly. We're here for you whatever happens."

I can't seem to find any words that make sense. I want my Mum, and Dad, and Pearl.

"Why were the funerals so quick?" is all I can think to ask.

More silence.

"We didn't know if you were going to survive Ocean. Every time I came to see you I was told not to get too hopeful. Everything was such a shock. I don't know. It seemed the best thing to do."

"So here I am three weeks after my sister dies and I can't even grieve properly." I raise my voice and then see the torment in Aunt Sophie's eyes.

I feel my own tears coming again.

Aunt Sophie puts her arms around me as I weep.

"We'll take one day at a time" she says eventually. "The doctors think you'll need to be in here for at least another month to build up your strength and do some initial physio. That gives us plenty of time to think about the future and for me to try and sort things out."

"But what about school?" I stammer. "I've got GCSE's coming up!"

"Ocean" says Aunt Sophie, "You can't worry about that yet. You need to get back on your feet..." She pauses awkwardly.

"You mean foot" I say, looking deeply into her eyes.

Aunt Sophie looks horrified for a moment. Then we both smile. Not a big smile, but it makes us both feel a little better.

Chapter 8

The following day a different nurse called Chloe comes into my room.

"Hi Ocean," she says in a sickly, patronising tone. "I'm going to be looking after you today. I'll also be helping our physiotherapist to get you upright, as you haven't sat up since your accident, have you?"

I shake my head, for two reasons:

1. I know it's true that I need to sit up again at some point.

2. It's only half eight in the morning and far too much for me to take in.

It's funny, before my accident I was a morning person most of the time. I'd always be up and ready to go by half seven. But now, I prefer to stay asleep, as long as I don't dream about the crash. It happens most nights. I just keep seeing her face, my face in reverse. Whenever I try and think about her, my heart physically hurts. I honestly think that half of me, the best half of me, has been ripped away.

Later on that morning there's a knock at the door to my single room. It's the first time it's happened since I've been here.

"Yes?" I say, trying to sound pleased as a result of this person's respect for my privacy.

A tall and pretty woman with long black dreadlocks opens the door and comes into my room.

"Hi there Ocean," she says. "My name's Bella and I'm going to be your physiotherapist."

I try and smile. Bella is honestly the first staff member who's spoken to me like a fourteen year old since I've been here. But the smile doesn't work, the pain of losing Dad and Pearl overpowers any feelings of joy.

"So," says Bella, "I'm going to slightly raise your head and I'll do it very gradually, like when you had your eye dressings taken off."

Bella raises my head using the bed control hooked over the side. She only raises it about ten degrees but it feels like a real shock to the system.

"I'll be back throughout the day to increase the level. OK?" asks Bella, her big brown eyes shining with kindness.

"OK," I say in a soft whispering voice.

It feels like the longest day ever. Bella comes in on about ten occasions throughout it, every time asking me with real, genuine compassion how I'm feeling, and I tell her. I tell her that I feel tired, I tell her that I feel like the sun will never come out again in my life and I tell her that I don't feel complete now that Pearl's gone. She listens and says the same words that Laura said to me a fortnight ago. But the way she says them sounds kinder and like they come from a deeper place. It feels like the words are more sympathetic than most people when they say *"I'm so sorry,"* and *"That sounds so difficult."*

By the evening I'm able to sit up straight. It feels, in a tiny way, somehow empowering. But it tires me out so much that I have to lie back down again after half an hour and close my eyes immediately.

"We'll work on it more tomorrow," says Bella, a smile clearly present in her voice.

The next morning, as promised, Bella helps me sit up for longer and longer time periods. It's the same every day for a week.

"Now," says Bella one morning, "Today I think we should try and get you transferred into a wheelchair."

I defiantly shake my head. I don't want to leave this bed. I don't want to sit in a chair on wheels because that means people can forcibly take me places. It also means people can see that I have part of my leg missing. In bed it's hidden.

"No?" echoes Bella sympathetically, clearly reading my mind. "All we'll work on today and for the next few days is transfering into the chair and sitting there for a few minutes."

"Transfering?" I repeat.

"Practicing getting into and out of bed, to and from your wheelchair without the use of one of your legs," she replies. She makes it sound matter of fact. *Without the use of one of your legs*.

She then picks up a piece of plastic shaped like a giant cashew nut.

"This is called a banana board."

The name does make sense.

"The way it works," says Bella, "Is I'll place one end of it on the side of your bed and then you can slide across. It may feel difficult at first as you've not used the majority of your muscles for quite a while. We'll practice it though and it will become more natural."

Easy! I think naively. Chloe carefully pulls back the sheets covering my lower body and I gasp. It's worse than I could have imagined. My once long and strong left leg is now an awkward, ugly stump, cut off below where my knee. My mirror image birthmark which connected me and Pearl together is now not visible (my skin is too raw) and my right leg is the same colour as what is left of my left leg. A new wave of emotion cascades over me, intensifying my grief. If this is what my lower body is now, probably the last bit of me to be burned, what must the rest of my body look like?

"I know," says Chloe, trying to sound nice, I guess, but just sounding patronising beyond belief, "It's a big shock but I'm sure you're still just as beautiful as you were before…"

Bulllshit! I think. *You have no idea what I looked like before this.*

I stay looking at my once Vogue-worthy legs, as Bella lowers my bed so that it is level with the wheelchair.

"Right," says Bella, "I want you to very gently and slowly shuffle your way towards the board."

I try but I wince as soon as I press weight through my still broken and casted left arm. The pain is too intense. Even when I try pushing through my right arm the pain is still too much.

"Try shuffling and pushing at the same time," suggests Bella.

I try and the pain is still unimaginable but eventually I'm sitting on the banana board.

"Now," says Bella, "Slide yourself over, it shouldn't be too difficult as your hospital gown won't create much friction."

I slowly slide myself into the wheelchair on the right hand side of my bed. Bella claps with genuine enthusiasm and it feels like a big achievement. But then the room starts spinning.

"I don't feel well," I announce.

Bella and Chloe quickly help me transfer back into my bed. I feel sick as a result of the unaccustomed movement.

"You've done so well," says Bella confidently. "And it will get easier every day, I promise."

I shake my head despondently. I've always trusted Bella ever since she started helping me but the energy required to sit in a wheelchair for more than two minutes feels like a mountain-moving task.

Chapter 9

The next morning I am able to sit in my chair for five minutes.

"Well done," says Bella, "That's more than double what you did yesterday."

The time I'm able to sit in my chair continues to increase and within a week I manage an entire hour in my chair. As a result of this Helena decides that I need to get out of my room.

I start to panic about going beyond these four walls. I must look horrendous. I haven't actually seen myself in a mirror since my accident, but I just know that I look awful. Regardless, ten minutes later I'm being wheeled out of my room into the brightly lit corridor of the hospital's burns department. I realise that I've forgotten how loud the outside world is. All I can think is that people must be looking at my missing leg and hair.

A nurse called Emma wheels me to the other end of the ward, by which point I am completely one hundred percent knackered. So she wheels me back and I slide back into bed with the banana board, which has actually become far easier than it was the first time. So that's why, when Emma says in her strong Newcastle accent

"It'll get easier pet."

I one hundred percent believe her.

"I'll come check on you in a bit," she says, her brown eyes shining.

It's at that moment something catches the corner of my eye. I see a blank piece of paper and a biro resting on the mini chest of drawers next to my bed. I lean over and grab them with my right hand, which feels more natural than ever. I wonder if I'll still use my left arm once it comes out of plaster tomorrow. I pull my table on wheels over and I start to sketch.

I draw myself and Pearl, long hair down and wavy, blowing in all directions. I draw her… and myself… as I remember us looking: long, slim, strong. With the bodies of a pair of twins who adored dance classes. We mixed it up: ballet, tap, jazz, modern, hiphop. I really miss dance. I'll never be able to dance in the same way again. It's unbearable. I look back down at the sketch.

I miss Pearl… oh God… I miss her so much.

"Where are you?" I whisper. "I need you. Where the hell are you when I need you most?"

At this point my brain plays the same old cruel trick on me creating a subliminal response. I can almost hear her saying

That's such a good drawing. You're so talented. I'm not far away but at the same time I'm in a complete other realm.

I shake my head quickly. I can't really hear her voice and I will never hear her voice, or Dad's, but my brain creates a similar auditory illusion of him speaking softly.

You should really consider a career in art Ocean.

When Emma comes in to do my blood pressure and obs she gasps at my drawing.

"Ocean! That's so good. You have a real talent. Who's this other girl standing next to you? she asks.

"She's my twin" I say flatly.

"You're identical?"

"Yes."

"What's her name?"

"It's... it was Pearl," I say, tears brimming in my eyes. "She died in the accident where I got these burns and broke my arm and had my leg amputated. My Dad too!"

It feels odd saying it out loud. I realise I actually haven't done that since my accident.

"Oh Ocean," says Emma, looking shocked. "I'm so sorry."

I shake uncontrollably. The grief is no better than it was when I first regained consciousness. In fact, it's only really now starting to sink in that Dad and Pearl are gone. They're gone and they're never coming back.

Chapter 10

The next day the dreaded thing happens: being moved to an open ward. An open ward with a lot more noise!

"We're going to take your bed there now," says Laura, on duty for the first time since taking annual leave.

A porter comes and opens the door to my room so that the bed can fit through. Then he comes round and helps Laura and Emma wheel my bed round to the childrens' main ward. There are about nine other beds in the ward that I can see, but it appears to go on forever. My bed is rolled down the long room and then steered round a corner and taken right to the very end. It's parked next to a window and opposite a sleeping girl, who actually looks like a pretty similar age to me. It hits me at this moment that everyone else has a parent with them and I don't.

"I'll be back in about an hour to take you to get that cast removed," says Emma, giving me a nod and a smile. "And then in the coming weeks you can work with Bella to get that arm strong again and get yourself onto some crutches."

Crutches. Oh God. Then I'll really look like someone who's missing a leg.

"Thank you," I say softly. Emma, like Bella, is one of the few people in here who doesn't talk to me like I've got severe brain damage.

I look out of the window. It's surprising how much the seasons have changed since I've been here. Summer into Autumn. The trees have fiery red leaves and some have dropped already, speckling the green of the grass with tiny, bright infernos.

As promised, one hour later Emma comes back and I slide into my wheelchair.

"You ready?" she asks, positioning herself behind me.

"Yes," I nod.

She wheels me out of the ward, down corridors and into lifts and I start having hazy flashbacks. I think I remember voices.

She's seizing… Oxygen dropping… Going into shock.

I shake my head quickly and the flashbacks become less vivid.

After about five minutes Emma wheels me into a department that says 'Orthopaedics' in big blue letters above a set of double wooden swing doors. While Emma goes to check me in I glance around the packed room. Little kids with broken arms stare at me. I touch my head, which is another thing that I haven't done since my accident, and I can understand why. There is no hair there. Instead it's just bald, sore skin.

It takes me a while to take this in. No hair, none, all burned off in the accident. I remember mum telling me once that hair simply can't grow over scar tissue. So that means I'll be left bald for eternity. Since my accident my injuries appear to be like an onion, revealing endless layers and making your eyes water as the gas is released.

The department is very busy. Emma sits with me for an hour and a half, which is the longest time I've sat in a chair since I came here. Eventually though, I'm called into a room with a smiling doctor.

"Hello there Ocean," he says in a soft Greek accent. "So today we're going to send you for an x-ray. Then, fingers crossed, get that cast removed."

He gives us an x-ray form and begins to point Emma in the direction of the department but she interjects

"Uhm, Constantine, it's okay. I do work here."

"Oh, yes of course," he says, looking embarrassed.

They stay looking at each other for a second and exchanging: *It's fine, honestly, don't worry*, and *Okay then*, but eventually Emma begins wheeling me out of the department.

Another half hour passes waiting for an x-ray. I remember Mum going on and on about the NHS being underfunded and now I understand what she meant. For the time I waited I feel a bit shortchanged by how quick my x-ray is. It's done in like two minutes!

Rude!

We sit in the Orthopaedic department again, but not for as long this time. When I'm called back in to see Constantine (or whatever I'm meant to know him as), he has a smile on his face, which must seriously hurt to wear the whole time.

"It's fixed," he says. "The bone appears to have healed very nicely, so I'm going to send you to get that cast off in the plaster room," he says pointing to a room almost directly opposite.

"You shouldn't have to wait too long," he says, "They're quite efficient."

Luckily, he's right and we only have to wait five minutes for the technician. The machine that takes off my cast buzzes, slowly and deliberately, as it chews through my pink plaster cast. I feel slightly pissed off that none of my school friends have been able to sign it. I remember when Hafsa broke her wrist we all signed her cast and when Madeline broke her leg we all signed that too. But I only have one signature from Bella on mine and that's cut through by the machine. Once my shoulder-high cast is completely off, I try to bend my elbow. Big mistake. It jolts up suddenly and sends shooting pains along the entire limb.

"That can happen," says the technician, "But it'll get better in about a week. If you keep bending and stretching, it'll start to feel more natural."

I nod. I know from the physiotherapy I've done so far that Bella is no pushover and that even if I'm struggling like mad to do my exercises, she will help me get through them, gently, slowly but surely.

By the time Emma has pushed me back to the ward my eyes feel like lead and keep closing. Aunt Sophie was right, it really is going to take a while to build up my strength. When I get back to my bed I fall straight asleep and stay asleep for two hours (despite all the noises around me). When I wake up the girl opposite is awake. She has a huge burn running from her left hand to her right hand. All the skin on her neck looks scaly and sore. I give her a small smile. She looks up for a second and gives a coy smile in response, before pushing her mousy hair behind her ear and looking back down at her phone.

Chapter 11

I feel uplifted when Aunt Sophie visits again the next morning. She can't stay long as she is going to watch Jack in his Halloween Pumpkin Dance at school.

Whatever!

It's so nice to talk to someone who knows me and after she leaves I twiddle my hospital wrist band. I read it again and again. Ocean Rodrigo, 26th January, 2004. I stare at it for a long time and wonder how they know all this about me. I think Mum may have mentioned how they identify people after accidents but I honestly can't remember.

My mind continues to wander about with no real purpose. There's not really much else to do when you're stuck in a hospital ward. I also do some more sketching on scrap pieces of paper. Since my accident there's been so much negative energy building up inside of me. The only way I can get rid of it is by drawing. It's never really anything specific, sometimes the sunset, a duck, a woman I once saw on the bus. Somehow it feels like the pen helps me slowly get rid of some of the pain of losing Dad and Pearl. It's strange, people say these things get better with time, but the pain seems to run slightly deeper everyday as it feels less and less like a nightmare that I will wake up from soon, and more and more like a harsh, tense, painful new reality.

Yesterday I caught sight of myself in the lift mirror on the way back up to the ward and gasped at my new appearance. My once pale, smooth, porcelain skin is now an army of angry, red scars. I look so different that it took me a second to realise that I was looking at my new physical identity. My mind keeps flashing back to the accident and the big smile Pearl wore minutes before her life was cut short by a wrong turning which went even more wrong. Her soft, sweet voice that was always so unbelievably calm, collected and gentle, whatever the situation.

My mind continues to wander onto new subjects. What would Pearl be like if she'd survived? She'd cope with it far better than me. But then my mind starts screaming.

But she did die… she's gone… and she didn't survive, and these words in my head repeatedly stab me again and again like a dagger.

That night I lie in my bed for ages but I can't fall asleep. The ward is so big that there's someone being sick or having a fit or something every twenty minutes or so. As soon as I manage to drop off a nurse comes and checks my observations and I'm woken up again by the squeezing of the blood pressure cuff. Sometimes the machine struggles to get a reading and the machine squeezes harder. It squeezes so hard that I feel like my arm might come off.

The next morning the ward starts bustling around properly at half seven, still far too early since my accident. I can see once I've sat up that the girl opposite me taps away on her phone, like she did yesterday. I miss the smooth light feeling of holding my iPhone. I miss my friends. I realise that I've had nil contact with the real outside world since my accident and I'm suddenly craving social interaction.

I wonder what they've been told at school, if anything? Do they know that I'm now missing one leg and I've got burns everywhere? Do they know that my sister, my twin, is dead?

I try to imagine Miss Collins telling my year group what has happened to me. What did she say?

Now, you may have noticed that Pearl and Ocean Rodrigo haven't been in, well... I shake my head.

Time drags on, but moves very quickly at the same time, and before I know it it's eight thirty in the evening. The lights have been off for about an hour but I decide to turn my lamp on and sketch. I draw a line down the piece of paper. On one side I draw the feeling of life if Pearl had lived, swirls, stars, hearts. On the other side I draw the feeling of life without Pearl. I draw rain, hearts with zigzagged cracks through them, empty boxes, because that's how it feels: empty. I don't feel inspired to draw much more. That's the thing about creativity, sometimes it's there and other times it's not.

I'm so unbelievably tired, I don't know why though. All I've done today is sit, think, sketch and wonder how I'm going to carry on. Eventually sleep drags me down. But of course I keep being brought back to consciousness by nurses coming to check my blood pressure and stuff.

Chapter 12

It doesn't feel like long before I've weaved my way into and out of sleep for another night. About half way through the morning, a doctor who I don't recognise comes in with a nurse I don't recognise either.

"Hello there, Ocean," he says. "My name is Doctor Colden and I've been caring for your mother."

I've sort of stopped thinking about Mum. Everything's so hard to take in. What are we, end of September? I haven't seen her for nearly two months. I stop breathing for a second.

Oh God. Please don't tell me she's died too.

"What's happened to her? Is she okay?" I gabble frantically.

"Well, as you know she was very seriously injured. At times, in the first few weeks, it was very much touch and go whether or not she'd pull through. But miraculously her vital signs are starting to improve and we're hoping to be able to take her off life support this morning."

"Life support?" I ask.

"As I said," says Doctor Colden, "She was very seriously injured. So bad in fact, she's been in an induced coma ever since the accident."

I try to imagine being in that white, cloudy, nowhere-land for almost two whole months. But my mind can't seem to grasp that.

"I thought you might like to know that we're going to slowly reduce the anaesthetic. But don't expect her to be the same person she was before the accident. She's suffered massive trauma in the crash and she had a major bleed on the brain and we also think the frontal lobe is damaged."

"Frontal lobe?" I question.

"It's the part of the brain that controls consciousness so I'm afraid that we don't really know whether she'll fully recover."

I remember Mum helping me with my biology homework on the brain in year eight. I remember her telling me how life threatening 'an intracranial bleed' (as she called it) can be.

"I want to see her!" I say trying to stop the tears from rolling down my face. Doctor Colden opens his mouth and looks like he's about to say something but then his pager goes off and he rushes off.

"Excuse me," he says , leaving me with the unknown nurse.

Throughout the day I think and think about poor Mum. I worry that she might be in unbearable pain. I wonder how long it'll be before she finds out that I'm the only other survivor of the accident.

How different will she be? Will she be able to walk? Talk? Will she even know who I am? Know my voice?

I wonder how much her life will be affected by the accident. I realise that she'll probably not be able to practice medicine again; medicine, which she loved so much. She said that most days, when she went into work, she felt as though she'd made a difference to someone's life, and now her career, which she studied so hard for, could be over for ever.

So worrying about Mum is added to my thought loop that plays on repeat for the next two hours. It goes on and on and on, so I decide to do some sketching to try and free my mind from this mental prison. I draw how trapped I feel: tied up in a sack, in an iron cage, hanging threateningly off a cliff. If this was really happening I'd be counting my breaths, praying and waiting for the whole thing to be over. But instead I'm trapped in this hospital bed, unable to walk, covered in burns and worst of all without Dad and Pearl. If she were here we might be in beds next to each other. Time would feel normal and we wouldn't be bored even without our phones.

That afternoon Doctor Colden comes back, and he looks quite happy.

"So Ocean," he says. "Your Mum is doing very well off the anaesthetic. It'll be ok for you to visit her soon."

This is some weight off my chest but I still worry,

"Do you know how bad the damage is yet?" I ask.

Doctor Colden shakes his head.

"It's too early to tell. But I'll let you know once we know more."

I nod.

"Thank you."

Chapter 13

The next morning begins, as ever, with ward round, which is basically where a whole lot of random doctors come round to discuss your condition. While she's being examined, the girl opposite starts crying out in pain.

"She's really sore," says the woman I've assumed is her Mum.

"We'll get some extra pain relief prescribed," says the lead doctor.

When a nurse returns a bit later to administer the drugs she asks the girl for her wrist band.

"Can I ask your name please?" she says, in a half jokey voice. You get used to this routine in hospital, everytime they give you something.

"Maris Lyons. 1st of September 2004," she says.

I chuckle slightly. If there's one thing you learn in hospital, it's saying your date of birth! She must notice me laugh, because she looks across and beams at me.

"Hi Maris" I say. "I'm Ocean."

"Nice to meet you, Ocean," says Maris.

However, that's about as far as my good humour extends right now and I start to sketch another drawing. I draw how I feel my future will be: I draw myself shivering on a torture-like bench, with nails and shards and broken glass ominously glaring out. I draw my eyes wide and wondering, my body stick thin and covered in cuts and bruises from spending so many empty nights sleeping on the bench. My future could be as bleak as this, or worse. There is simply no way of being able to tell what it holds. When I was younger I wished there was a mirror which I could look into and see myself, what I would look like, at different ages. The age I mainly wanted to see myself at was the age of fourteen. But now I'm glad this mirror doesn't exist. If it did, my eight year old self would probably have nightmares as bad as the ones which roam my sleep now.

Later on that day Maris gets a visit from a family friend. She is given a super cute blue, flowing top.

"It'll be light on your burns," says the friend.

"Thank you so much," says Maris, smiling a toothy grin. Maris, her Mum and their friend talk for ages about the most mundane stuff like the weather and sleep deprivation and Christmas.

"One month till the countdown begins," squeals Maris excitedly.

One month? It can't be November yet can it? Have I really been here for that long?

After Maris's friend has left and her Mum has gone to grab some coffee, I decide to try and make conversation with her.

"Nice top," I say pointing to her new, cerulean blue tee shirt.

"Do you like it?" she says, sounding surprised.

"Are you kidding?" I say, "It's stunning!"

"I don't like blue. I prefer orange."

"Fair enough," I say nodding. "I love blue."

"Do you want it?" asks Maris, holding the top out in front of her.

"Sorry, what?" I say, taken aback.

"Do you want the top? You do look like blue suits you," she says. " And you don't seem to have many clothes with you," Maris says slowly. "If you don't mind me asking, what happened to you?"

I sarcastically laugh and shake my hands in front of my face.

"Sorry," she says apologetically. "I s'pose what I really mean is how did it happen to you?"

I take a deep breath and then say,

"Car crash. My twin sister and Dad were killed. My Mum still hasn't woken up and we don't know how bad her brain damage is." I'm trying hard to fight the tears from rolling down my face like they so often do when I least expect.

Maris gasps.

"Oh I'm so sorry." she says.

"What about you?" I struggle, "How did it happen to you?"

"An oil burn." says Maris. "I was trying to make some fried bread and a load of oil sprayed out at me about a month ago," she says, shaking with the memory of the trauma.

"What was she called?... Your... your sister?" gabbles Maris.

"Pearl." I say softly. "Her name was Pearl."

I start talking about my twin. I tell her how Pearl always cared about others, how she had a laugh which filled you with the most amazing warm glow. For the first time it feels good to be talking about Pearl even though the anguish is still there. I feel like I could describe her forever. At that moment though, Maris's Mum comes back and we have to stop talking. It almost feels as if Pearl is a secret I can only share with Maris, for now. I scribble on a piece of paper and turn it round to show Maris. "*Speak later?*" it reads. She nods and gives a thumbs up.

I now draw another sketch, this time of Pearl. I draw myself looking sad but with her by my side. It's just her and me but that one other person seems to make all the difference. I draw big goofy smiles across our faces. I even draw myself with some of my leg missing - it feels… more honest somehow. We look happy and like we're having a good time, whatever we're doing. I decide it's my best drawing since coming here. I squint at the page for ages and make my hands take turns to draw parts of the picture as I am now completely ambidextrous. It also creates a kind of smooth sophisticated style to the picture.

About two hours later Doctor Colden strides in.

"Hello there Ocean," he says, "How are you doing?"

He gestures at my sketch.

"This is amazing!" he exclaims "You have a real talent."

"Thanks," I say, as I glance thoughtfully down at my drawing.

"I've come to talk to you about your Mum" says Doctor Colden.

Chapter 14

I'm wheeled by a porter called Priti into room four of the neuro injury ward. A nurse called Leroy follows behind. The door of the single isolation room is opened. The lights are fairly dim in this room. Despite the low lighting, my keen eye can make out a bed. At first all I can see is a spaghetti junction of tubes and wires. But then I see her. Her eyes are taped shut, her pale face is thin, boney and gaunt. Her once long luscious hair is now considerably shorter and tied back in a top knot. She has wires, providing oxygen to her damaged brain, coming out of both nostrils. Her lips are set in an expressionless, thin line.

Will she always look this way? This is terrible.

No longer strong, independent, capable.

Instead helpless, broken, damaged.

Is she even the same person?

This is worse than I ever could have imagined.

Priti wheels me over to the side of her bed so I can gently take her pale hand in mine.

"We'll leave you with her for a bit," says Leroy, "to talk to her."

Leroy and Priti walk through the door and gently shut it behind them. I take a deep breath and open my mouth.

What am I going to say?

"Hey Mum," I say softly, my voice audibly shaking. "It's me… it's Ocean," I whisper.

"Mum?" I continue, a lump forming in my throat.

"I don't even know if you can hear me. I don't even know if you can remember me. I don't even know if you'll ever fully wake up from this. But I just want you to know that I love you so much. You're an amazing Mum and I'll always love you."

Mum remains expressionless.

Is there any point?

Earlier Dr Colden told me the grim news. That the damage to her brain means she'll always drift in and out of consciousness.

"I'm sorry but there's very little we can do to bring her back to how she was prior to the accident."

The words hurt. They hurt not just because I've essentially lost my Mum, my Mum, the only close family I've got left, but because she'll be trapped in a constant sleepy cycle for the rest of her life. I personally think that she's had a worse outcome than Dad and Pearl.

I sit with Mum for about an hour telling her about the pictures I've been drawing and about how I love her so much and all that super cringey stuff. Eventually though I feel so tired. I feel like I could slump forward and fall straight to sleep. So I'm taken back to the ward and transfer back onto my bed. I look across the ward to Maris's bed. She's smiling and gently putting a black puffer coat around her body. She walks over to me.

"Hi Ocean," she says softly.

"Hi," I say looking up at her. She's very tall.

"Why are you wearing a coat?" I ask.

"I'm going home," says Maris, "I'm really going to miss you."

She then rummages inside her pocket and brings out an iPhone 6.

"Look," she says, "I know you don't have a phone any more. So I want you to have my old phone."

She holds out the phone to me.

"Mum bought me the iPhone X as an early Christmas present. If you get a pay as you go sim it should work fine."

I'm not sure how to get a pay as you go sim or even if I have any money or who is going to look after me.

"I don't know if I can," I gabble quickly.

"Yes you can," says Maris "Take it… Please take it."

"Thank you," I say, genuinely touched by the kindness of this girl I barely know. "Thank you so much."

Maris leans forward and gives me a huge but gentle hug and I wrap my arms around her.

Sometimes people you only meet once have an amazing effect on your life.

Chapter 15

Later that afternoon I'm visited by Aunt Sophie.

"Sorry I haven't been to see you in a while," she says, "Jack and Holly have had the norovirus and I've been up to my eyes in disinfectant. Anyway, enough about my problems, how are you?"

"I'm doing alright in some ways," I say, "But not so well in others."

"Do you want to talk about it?" says Aunt Sophie sitting down on a chair next to my bed. I shake my head defiantly.

"No," I say.

"Oh," says Aunt Sophie, taken aback. "Uhm, that's fine."

"Did you draw this?" she asks, doing her best to change the subject.

"Uhm... yeah," I stumble.

"This is fantastic!"

"Thanks," I say bluntly.

Aunt Sophie and I continue this seesaw exchange for forty five minutes. We talk about a wide variety of things. Things like, Christmas, hospital life and Aunt Sophie's work related dramas. At some point she tells me it's looking likely that I'll be coming to live with her, Jack, Holly and Aunty Rose. I don't know how I feel about that but I need to live somewhere and mum isn't going to be able to be a legal guardian.

One day at a time.

"It'll be nice to have an uninterrupted night's sleep," is all I can think to say.

"While we're on the topic," says Aunt Sophie, "One of us, me or Aunty Rose, is going to go and grab some of your things from your house for when you move in. You know, to make the spare room feel more homely. And what colours do you like? We're going to decorate your room for you."

I haven't really thought about my old house much. It hits me hard when Aunt Sophie mentions it so casually.

"Clothes? Well, just comfy stuff for now," I say. "And for my room I'm thinking like most of the walls painted sky blue and the chimney breast painted an orange?" I suddenly experience a rare feeling of optimism and start to describe my dream bedroom with beaded white hangings coming down from the ceiling and a blackout blind, so I'm not woken up by the sun every morning. She makes notes on her phone and says things like:

"Uhu," and "Sounds stunning. We'll do our best."

She gives me a big hug and is about to leave, saying she'll return soon, when she whips back round to face me, reaches into her bag and brings out a little credit card of some sort.

"It's a new sim-card that came for you today. I know your phone was lost in the accident..." She pauses, once again succumbing to a wave of realisation, the kind of wave that's been hitting me constantly ever since I first woke up and realised what's happened to me.

"I haven't had time to get a new phone for you yet," she continues, composing herself again, "But the phone company sent the card through anyway."

"That's OK" I say. "Fortunately a friend here has given me her old iPhone."

Thank you Maris!

It's been a lot to take in. But at least I now have a sim card. I borrow a paper clip from the doctor's clipboard and insert it.

Actually feel excited.

I unlock the phone, which feels light in my hands, and delete all Maris's contacts. I then sign into Instagram, knowing my account name and password off by heart.

There are some things you just can't forget.

I check my DMs. There are 125 unread messages! I scroll through messages like *"Hey Ocean I miss you,"* from Madeline and *"Can't wait till you're better,"* from Hafsa and *"Thinking of you,"* from Daisy in my year.

I spend the next hour replying to every single message. It's strange how much anxiety is caused by reading through so many get-well-soon messages. It makes me wonder how close to death I was. I imagine myself looking like Mum, eyes taped shut, face pale and pasty. But at the same time it reminds me that life carries on outside the hospital and that the world still turns without me. I'm actually quite inconsequential in the grand scheme of things.

I honestly cannot describe how it feels to be tapping on a phone again. At first it feels quite unnatural but my fingers soon remember every step to the texting dance. I download Netflix, hoping that we still have an account. Luckily we do, so I am able to binge watch all the shows I've missed: *Glee, Derry Girls, The Office* and *Stranger Things*

Watching TV has never felt better. It feels like a warm and fluffy cloud, soft, friendly and familiar.

Chapter 16

The next morning Bella comes to my bedside holding two crutches.

"Right Ocean," she says, "Today we're going to work on your upper body strength so that eventually you can hop using these crutches. I'll start with the most obvious thing." She picks up the electrical control for my bed.

"We're first going to build up to you being able to sit up unsupported," she continues.

I realise that I've only done this for like five seconds when sliding from my bed to my chair and like most things since the accident they need to be one hundred percent relearned. Right now hospital seems to be more about rehabilitation than recovery. Every day I have to work hard at something I previously would not have thought twice about. After about a minute of sitting with no support, my stomach hurts, like how it used to hurt after I did an abdominal workout before my accident; and about a minute after that every part of my body is shaking with the effort of sitting up.

Thanks Bella - not!

Over the next two weeks I keep working on my core strength. It starts at a low level but towards the end of the time period I'm able to quite easily lift two kilogram weights and do five sit ups one after another. By mid December I can hop quite some distance around the ward. So a week before Christmas I am visited by a social worker called Amanya.

"Now Ocean," she begins, "As you know, the doctors want you to go home soon. And I know it's been agreed that your

Aunt Sophie will take on your guardianship. It's going to be a big change leaving here after what you've been through" says Amanya. "You have to try and be patient with your new family and yourself. We'll be supporting you as much as we possibly can, but the psychological effects of what you've been through are going to take a while."

She's absolutely right. The psychologists have incrementally increased my antidepressants and I'm now on the top dose, but neither time nor fluoxetine have made me feel anything other than still-depressed so far.

Later I draw how I feel about being in a home-like setting again. I draw a mixture of hearts and rain around me. It will be nice to be surrounded by loved ones again, but at the same time… Pearl's not there. I make a mental note to ask for some proper art materials for Christmas. I'm bored to death of the limitations of a biro and scrap paper. The sketches I've been drawing for the last few months lack depth and real character.

Finally the day arrives. Just before Christmas Aunt Sophie comes to take me home. Once the paperwork is completed I'm free to leave. The hop down to Aunt Sophie's car feels like a marathon, which I am determined to finish without help. When I get outside the British winter air hits me like a million small pellets, even though I don't think it's even that cold. I breathe in the air filled with petrol fumes and cigarette smoke, which makes me briefly cough.

"You okay?" asks Aunt Sophie, looking concerned. I nod, having forgotten how it feels to be outside in the big wide world.

Aunt Sophie helps me into her silver car. Panic rises in my chest, as flashbacks of the last time I sat inside one race through my head. Seeing the apprehension in my eyes, once she's got into the driver's seat, Aunt Sophie says soothingly,

"I promise it won't happen. Now," she says, turning the engine on, "Let's get you home."

I smile as Aunt Sophie slowly drives out of the hospital car park. Aunt Sophie and Aunty Rose actually live very close to my old home but Aunt Sophie takes a detour so I don't need to confront the phantoms of the past by travelling down my old street. *Our street, mine and Pearl's. Not anymore.* I can't deal with that yet.

Once we arrive at my Aunties', it feels strange entering into a building that smells of washing powder and fresh cooking, as opposed to one that smells strongly of bleach and stomach-churning, tinned hospital food. The walls in the entrance hall are painted a tasteful cream with photos and art work on the wall. I realise, in this one moment, that I have seriously missed being in a home environment.

"Let's look at your new room" says Aunt Sophie, nodding towards the door where the spare room used to be.

I pause.

Aunt Sophie opens the door to my new space.

I gasp.

The walls are my favorite blue and the chimney breast is painted in a vibrant orange. The bed and duvet cover look wonderfully homely after hospital and the new paint smells so fresh. *Wow!* I also can't miss a hand drawn sign stuck to the wall just above the mantelpiece WELCOME HOME OCEAN it says, in big childish handwriting. *Holly!*

"We haven't managed the beads yet but we've put a blackout blind in so hopefully you'll get some good rest."

I feel so emotional I can't really speak.

"Come on," says Aunt Sophie warmly, "Let's get you sat down in the lounge."

The tall Christmas tree, as always, stands in the middle of their sitting room. It's lovingly decorated with a mixture of baubles and home-made wonky-eyed snowmen, made from pieces of carefully cut out card.

I imagine what our Christmas tree would have been decorated with. I imagine the annual third of December tradition of putting up all the decorations, with Michael Buble's Christmas CD playing in the living area. Pearl loved Christmas. She'd always put so much effort into the gifts she gave. She'd start planning all the Christmas presents in mid November. She was the exact opposite from me, rushing out at half three in the afternoon on Christmas Eve.

Aunt Sophie comes back into the lounge, from the adjoining kitchen.

"Do you want a cup of tea?" she asks, "Or a chocolate Christmas biccie?" It's so clear my aunt has young children: using words like *"biccie"*. I shake my head.

"No thanks, I'm not hungry right now."

"Alright then," says Aunt Sophie. "Well how about I find a Christmas film or something for you to watch."

I nod. It'll be nice to have a chilled afternoon. I find a new Christmas film called *The Christmas Chronicles* on Netflix. It's only been out a few weeks. It's about a brother and sister who mess up Santa's sleigh and have to pull an all-nighter to help him get Christmas back on track. It's just a kid's movie but I enjoy watching it, as I snuggle under the warm fluffy blanket on the light blue sofa.

When the credits start rolling, Aunt Sophie comes back in from her office where she's been catching up on some work.

"Aunty Rose will be back with Jack and Holly soon." She pauses. "Don't be surprised if they act a bit... shocked when they see you. Okay?"

I nod. I would understand if my younger cousins felt nervous about seeing me. They're used to seeing a tall, athletic teen, with long blond hair; and not a teen with no hair and burns everywhere that can be seen. It freaked me out the first time I saw myself, and I'm almost fifteen! I try to imagine how I'd have reacted when I was five or seven, but I can't. I can't imagine what they'll think.

Chapter 17

When they arrive back, it's clear that Holly and Jack *are* shocked, but they try to hide it.

"What happened to your leg Ocean" asks Holly, "Did they put it in recycling?"

"Well…" I begin.

"Or did they feed it to the lions at the zoo?" asks Jack.

I snap my fingers in front of my face.

"Yes, that's definitely it," I say.

We laugh for a bit and it seems to break the ice.

They tell me all about the last day of the term and how they made paper snowflakes, which is something I remember making at primary school. I miss primary school. I miss the feeling that when you go back to school after being ill for a week, there's nothing to catch up on. It'll take me forever to catch up with my work now.

I realise that Holly and Jack can't take their eyes away from where part of my leg used to be. I feel like I'll never get over it myself so how can I expect other people to adapt quickly especially when they are as young as Holly and Jack. Suddenly, Holly starts sniffling. It's quiet to start with but increases in volume very quickly.

"What's the matter my angel?" asks Aunty Rose sweetly.

"I want Pearl," Holly says softly.

Aunty Rose looks up to me with a sympathetic / encouraging look.

"Well…" I say, "I miss her too. I think we'll all miss Pearl and my Dad."

I can barely say the words.

They all look sadly into the middle distance for a moment. But then, pulling herself together, Aunt Sophie sniffs and then says, in a slightly shaky voice,

"I don't think Uncle Max, Aunty Millie or Pearl would want us to stay sad forever. They'd want us to enjoy Christmas."

I know she's trying, but I can tell she's in agony inside because her sister is still here, but not here at the same time. Her sister, who she loves so much, will never be able to laugh with her or have a conversation with her again. I know that my aunt feels the same way I do, like a part of her has been ripped away suddenly and without any warning. She feels the same empty ache inside, which seems like it will never go away no matter how much time passes.

That evening we make Christmas biscuits and then ice them before hanging them on the tree. They just add to the homely, festive feel of the happy home, which I suppose is now my home. Holly and Jack seem to have rallied and are no longer looking at my non-leg as I scoot around the room with my ever increasing crutch-skills.

"I'm putting a snowman on my biscuit," says Jack happily.

"What are you going to put on yours Ocean?"

"I'm not really sure," I say, "Maybe a snowflake?"

"I'm going to put Rudolf on mine!" exclaims Holly, her big blue eyes filled with excitement.

That night I sleep like a log. Not only because the mattress is soft, comfortable and welcoming, but also because it's an uninterrupted night. It's empty of machines beeping, or the sound of a baby two beds down crying out in pain. I'm just alone with my grieving dreams. It feels like I finally have the

head space to compute that Pearl, my sister, is never going to
come back.

Chapter 18

I'm woken at seven a.m. the next day as Holly comes skipping into my room.

"Ocean?" she calls, as she dives into the empty space in the double bed, "Ocean? Are you awake?"

"Yes, yes, I'm awake now, yes," I yawn.

"Ocean, can you tell me a story."

I cringe. Pearl was the story teller. It was honestly never my forté but I take a deep breath in and give it my best shot.

"Once upon a time, in a land far away there was a beautiful mermaid called Holly." I turn to my cousin to see if I'm doing this right. She nods impatiently.

"Yes!!! Carry on with the story!"

"Holly lived with her best friend Puppet The Clownfish and her two Mums Sophie and Rose. She also had a brother called Jack."

I carry on like this for about ten minutes, telling the story about how Holly The Brave Mermaid had to fight the Ocean Demon. Every time I mention the roaring, spiky demon Holly squeals and hides her face under the duvet. She even seems to be getting used to my lack of a limb as her hand accidentally clutches the stump as she laughs and screams at my story.

I spend some of the morning playing a Christmas board game with Holly and Jack. It would be the dullest game ever, but the excitement on my cousins' faces when they land on a 'lucky square' is absolutely priceless.

"I've landed on the magic reindeer," squeals Jack, on at least ten occasions.

"I've landed on the happy snowman," giggles Holly about fifteen times. I can't get over how adorable they are. They're little patches of sun on a depressingly, grey day.

Holly then asks me to plait her hair like I used to have mine. She moans and complains as I pull her feral mop into place but is really excited once it's done. Jack then asks me to do the same with his short, slightly scraggy hair. It's difficult but eventually he settles for a little man-bun.

That night I use some of Jack's partially dried out coloured felt-tip pens to draw how Christmas will feel at my new home, but without Pearl. I draw a Christmas tree with distressed looking reindeer decorations and melting almost flat, sad-looking snowmen. I draw the Christmas turkey with a visibly terrified scream on its face. I draw all the Christmas dinner trimmings as being mouldy and covered in fluffy, white penicillin bacterium. I draw the normally silver and gold cheery tinsel as being black and the colours of nightmares. I draw my aunties and cousins in tears on the sofa. I do my best, with the felt-tips, to draw outside as being wet instead of snowy. It most likely will be with climate change, which has been in the news quite a bit lately because of a Swedish school girl giving up her education to strike against the global issue. Finally I draw myself as a sad, decrepit, uneven shadow, with my infamous pair of crutches. I start to wonder how Christmas will actually be under the current circumstances.

I ponder this for a while.

Will the Christmas pop songs still sound the same to me?

Will the jokes in the crackers still make me laugh at how bad they are?

Will the chocolate taste the same?

I feel like I'm falling down, down, down in a world that I don't understand anymore. Christmas used to be the anchor but now I feel lost at sea.

Chapter 19

The next morning, I use my new debit card to do some online Christmas shopping. Aunt Sophie explained how she now has access to funds from my Mum and Dad and we agree a monthly allowance.

"I hadn't really thought about that before," says Aunt Sophie, "You know with Jack and Holly being so young. But I now realise that kids your age want money of their own to spend. I know I definitely did." She smiles.

For Aunt Sophie I buy a mug (for her caffeine addiction); for Aunty Rose I buy a cupcake cookery book, as I know she loves to bake and is always looking for new recipes; for Holly I buy a beginners' hair guide (so that she can improve on her hair-care skills); and for Jack I buy some felt-tip pens (to replace the ones I almost completely used up last night). I know that in the grand scheme of things I could have done tons better with my gift choices, but I'm sure they'll understand, given that I only came out of hospital two days ago. Let's hope they get here on time.

I spend the rest of the morning teaching Holly how to play *Uno* (the world's easiest game). Regardless though, it takes her like ten rounds to get the basic idea, and even after that point she keeps forgetting to say "Uno!" and has to pick up an extra two cards.

But whatever, she is only seven after all!

The next few days roll by in much the same way, everyday a perfect carbon copy of the last. Everyday is filled with laughter and Christmas movies and far too many mince pies. Every day is filled with Holly and Jack singing and dancing and telling bad jokes. Every day is filled with love and kindness and a kind of bittersweet feeling (for me anyway). Pearl, Dad and Mum should be here under this fleecy, fluffy blanket on the sofa. They should all be here looking at the twinkling Christmas tree with wrapped gifts underneath. I should be at home and we should be listening to Christmas songs. I try to join in but my laugh feels forced, my singing is all croaky and I can't seem to get in the mood.

On Christmas Eve the low-hanging, late December sun shines down on the thin layer of frost, which lies on the ground. Holly and Jack run around the house shouting:

"SANTA'S COMING! SANTA'S COMING! SANTA'S COMING!"

I smile at their innocence. I remember Pearl and I being this excited about Christmas. When we were little we used to do everything for Christmas; put mince pies and hot chocolate out for Father Christmas; put up our Christmas stockings and try and stay awake for the 'Big Jolly Man in his Big Red Suit.' Even when we stopped believing in all that stuff, Christmas was still always fun. But now, despite my aunties' best efforts, it feels empty. It feels like everything's wrong and can't be made right; and that's obviously because Christmas *is* wrong and it *can't* be made right. Christmas will be a tinsel-lined shadow of what it was last year.

Chapter 20

"It's Christmas!" screams Holly, at six a.m. the next morning.

"Santa's been!" shouts Jack.

I groan and pull the white duvet over my head. Is this what Christmas is like with young kids in the house? How the hell did my parents manage with me and Pearl when we were that age? It feels so unbelievably wrong that Pearl isn't here right now. My best friend, the person I loved (and still love) should be here right now and not in some cold scary graveyard. I roll over onto my left hip in the bed, still half asleep. That's when I see it. There's a big bulging blue stocking on the floor. Aunt Sophie and Aunty Rose have clearly thought of everything. I push myself up to sitting and plump the cushions behind my shoulders. I then pick up the heavy stocking and place it on the bed next to me.

I unwrap: three tubes of jelly beans (my favourite sweets), three packets of chocolate covered raisins (another Christmas classic) and a pink bobble hat. But then I unwrap a packet of pencils (of varying thicknesses), a tin of oil paints and a big A3 artists' drawing pad. A giant smile spreads across my face. I pull out a thin pencil and start sketching the outlines of a picture of winter happiness. I draw myself wearing the bobble hat with the long hair that once covered my back, wearing a warm winter coat. I stand next to a big Christmas tree. I start drawing Pearl but it doesn't look right so I am forced to rub her out with the other end of the pencil. I feel guilt spreading through my body. It feels like I'm rubbing her out of my life.

I try to draw her again and again on the next page but I keep having to rub her out. Have I forgotten what my sister looked like?

After a Christmas breakfast of croissants more presents are opened underneath the tree. I'm thinking that there wouldn't be anything more under there for me, what with all the generous gifts in the stocking, but Aunty Rose hands me a box-shaped silver package.

"I hope you like it," she says as I rip the paper open. "We just thought it might make going back to school a tiny bit easier."

Under the paper there's a black box with the word *Outre* on it.

"What the hell?" I think as I open the box. But then I gasp. Inside is a long blond wig, which looks pretty similar to how my hair used to look. There's also a wig cap and some kind of surgical tape.

"It's to help stick it down and stop it blowing away," explains Aunty Rose gesturing to the tape.

"Oh my goodness. Thank you so much, it's beautiful" I stammer. I didn't expect this much love and generosity, and the thoughtfulness of the wig makes me feel like crying. Fortunately I don't and manage to give my Aunties a big hug instead.

Holly breaks the tension by saying

"I thought Ocean would get a new leg, but hair is way better than that," and we all chuckle. Maybe you can get used to things if people around you are accepting.

I have a shower and get dressed. I then hop over to the mirror and sit down. I pick up the wig from the table next to the mirror. First I put the fabric wig cap on. It feels cool, safe and comfortable against my scarred skull. I then stick it onto my head using the tape. It feels a bit odd but I'm sure I'll get used to it. I then place the hair on top and let out a deep breath when I see myself in the mirror. I look more normal than I have since the crash. I brush the wig out on my head and it feels quite similar to how it felt to brush my own hair. I decide that when I go back to school (coz it'll have to happen at some point) I should definitely wear it.

Christmas lunch, a turkey with all the trimmings. I surprise myself by joining in with all the laughter, especially the Cringey Christmas Cracker jokes. I have to stop myself giggling when we get the inevitable Christmas dinner argument. It starts when Jack takes Holly's paper clip (her Christmas cracker toy).

"That's mine!!!" she yells. "Give it back." Holly reaches across the table and knocks over the big white jug of gravy.

"HOLLY!" shouts Aunty Rose, starting to lose her temper, "What do you say?"

"Sorry," says Holly, "But… but… he took my paper clip."

Aunty Rose rolls her eyes.

"Right Jack, can you give Holly her paper clip back please?"

"But I like it," defends Jack stubbornly.

"*Now* please," says Aunt Sophie sternly, and eventually Jack hands the paper clip back to Holly, who breaks it ten minutes later by repeatedly opening, closing, bending it out of shape and then clicking it back into line. The broken, cracked reindeer which was once on the end of the paper clip now lies semi-shattered on the white table cloth. This makes Holly burst into a flood of tears.

"That's alright darling," soothes Aunt Sophie, "You've got plenty of other lovely gifts".

This makes Holly nod and swallow back the sadness. After the white Christmas tablecloth, now covered in gravy and cracker bits, has been dispatched to the washing machine to be prepared for next Christmas I begin to fill colour into the dull world of pencilled outlines I created earlier. I paint my bobble hat as being pink and my coat a bright blue. I make my skin the colour it was before the accident, smooth and pale. I draw my eyes as being the same blue as the coat. I make the tree a deep olive green and paint tinsel and baubles on it. I paint the background as being a baby blue sky, the way it is just after it has snowed heavily.

"That's really good," says Aunty Rose when she walks into the kitchen, on the way to making herself and Aunt Sophie a mug of tea. I feel myself blushing and my eyes squinting with embarrassment. I wasn't like this before the accident; I was far more extrovert and outgoing. But now something's changed in my inner psyche.

"No really," continues Aunty Rose, "It's excellent."

That evening, I start to teach Holly how to do some basic hairstyles from the book I got her. It's got great pictures in it of some really complex hairstyles which she loves and points to.

"Can we learn that one Ocean?" she asks.

They look a bit tricky for her at this point so we start with a simple high ponytail from page one. It takes her half an hour to understand how much you have to brush the hair before you pull it up into the tie. She's so excited once she manages to tie an un-bumpy tail.

"Look!" she says, twirling in front of her Mums. "I did it all by myself," she giggles.

"Well done my angel," coos Aunty Rose, "You're doing so well."

Holly then tells me she wants to learn how to do Dutch Plaits.

"They look so pretty," she exclaims. But she can't understand that she has to split her hair into thirds and that she'll need to pull if she wants them to look good.

"Why can't I do it Ocean?" she sulks, sticking out her bottom lip and crossing her arms. I feel myself turning into a children's TV presenter as I say:

"It's alright, you're doing really well and you'll get there with lots of practice." This seems to be the sort of thing my baby cousin wants to hear and she cheers up very quickly, with the help of a couple of *Celebrations* chocolates!

Once I'm in bed I stare up at the ceiling in silent contemplation. Pearl, Dad and Mum should have been here today to share the fun with the family, because it was actually a very nice Christmas. They would've all thought that Jack and Holly's argument was very funny and the Christmas roast was deliciously tasty. They would have probably commented on my art work like Aunty Rose, and Mum and Dad would have got a little bit drunk in the evening like Aunty Rose and Aunt Sophie. I imagine Pearl trying to teach Holly how to do a ponytail instead of me. She would have been far less harsh and far more patient with our cousin when she didn't properly get all the hair into the tie, even though she wasn't very good with hair herself. She would have done the children's TV presenter impression far earlier in the hair schooling process. She would have smiled at Jack's drawing of an uneven snowman with arms poking from out of his square head. She would have cried at *The Snowman* movie, even though it's a kid's film which she's seen every Christmas since like forever! Pearl would have eaten loads of mince pies, but not quite enough to get a matching food-baby with me. She would have enjoyed Jack and Holly's Christmas snowflake dance and would have clapped even more enthusiastically than Aunt Sophie and Aunty Rose.

But the horrible truth is... Pearl couldn't share this magical Christmas with me. She can't laugh at the jokes in the Christmas crackers or excitedly open her presents. She won't ever be able to spend Christmas in a family home ever again. Because she's gone... she's gone... she's gone and she won't ever be coming back to life again.

Even though I know she isn't there, I whisper out into the darkness of the room

"Happy Christmas Pearl."

And my mind tells me what I want to hear back

"Happy Christmas Oceay."

Chapter 21

The next morning carries the usual anti-climactic wave of depression that Boxing Day always brings. It's a day when everyone's wanting to start their diets but there's so much sugary rubbish still left in the house from Christmas Day that it's basically impossible. The decorations are starting to look knackered - but maybe that's just me!

In my extended family's house though, they have an annual Boxing Day craft project, as Holly and Jack often get lots of kits for Christmas. I honestly think I had more fun than I've ever had on Boxing Day. I really enjoy painting tea coasters and decorating fabric canvas bags. I'd actually forgotten that craft sets like this even exist. I thought I was too old for activities such as putting freaky faces on socks and making them into sock puppets.

I was wrong.

"What's your puppet called, Ocean?" asks Holly, briefly looking up from sticking googly eyes on a pink sock.

"Mine's called..." she thinks for a second, "Spencer," she finally says, looking proud of herself.

I look down at the green sock I've covered with tiny pompoms and pipe cleaners. I decide he actually looks a bit like George's dinosaur from Peppa Pig, a show that Pearl and I were obsessed with when we were little.

"I think I'll call mine the Sockasaurus Rex," I declare, as I make the Sockasaurus Rex's eyes protrude from his face by sticking my fingers forward, which makes Holly squeal with half terror and half laughter.

"Hello," I say in a low silly voice. "My name's Sockasaurus Rex and I'm going to eat you up." This makes Holly and Jack hide under the table, shrieking.

"I would, except..." I continue, in the same pretend voice, "Except I'm a cousin of the Stegosaurus. So because of this I only eat plants."

This makes Holly and Jack breathe a sigh of relief and sit back up at the table to finish painting wooden picture frames in a very messy but charming style.

Later that day Aunt Sophie and I go to visit Mum in hospital. Although I know what I'm about to see, it doesn't make it any easier. I try telling her about Christmas and what a lovely time we had. I know she can't hear me but it feels right.

"She's now supporting her own breathing," explains the nurse, "So there's no need for her to still be here."

"Does that mean she can come home?" I ask hopefully.

The nurse shakes his head.

"No I'm afraid not. It means she'll probably be ready in the next week or so to move into a residential care home; we just need to find one that's..." he pauses, "Suitable for her."

I look at Mum in her hospital bed, most likely completely oblivious to Aunt Sophie and the nurse's conversation about 'Funding' and 'Twenty-four hours a day care' and 'Potential respiratory conditions.'

As I look down at my Mum's almost lifeless body, I realise that the chances of a complete recovery are miniscule.

When Aunt Sophie and I get back from the hospital, Holly wants me to try and teach her how to do Dutch Plaits on her hair again. She impatiently waits, quickly hopping from one foot to the other, as I have a cup of tea and the last mince pie.

"Come on Ocean!" she whines, "Hurry up! Come on!"

To be completely honest I'm glad of the distraction from my visit to Mum but I'm also starting to run out of patience. Was I honestly this hyper when I was seven? I begin to think my parents were more saintly than I ever realised before. After what seems like the hundredth cycle of "Come on Ocean!" I get up from the table and follow Holly to her room. I'm still not quite able to keep up with Holly using my crutches. But hey! What other choice do I have?

I'm actually pleasantly surprised when Holly reaches behind her hair and makes two clumsy plaits. Holly's handy work actually looks pretty similar to Pearl's first, and last, attempt at plaiting. My twin could never master the quick and subtle movements required to tie her hair. So once I was good enough at doing it, Pearl would make me do her hair every single morning. Five minutes before school she'd ask me to do top knots, plaits, buns, ponytails, fishtails and so much more. So I'm not going to lie, I became a bit of a pro!

"That's great," I say to Holly, trying to stop my voice from catching at the memory. "Keep practicing. That's ace!"

Holly honestly could not look any more happy than she does at this moment. Her smile gets bigger than any smile I've seen since the accident.

"Wow!" say Aunty Rose and Aunt Sophie as Holly pirouettes into the sitting room with her two plaits flying around, the way mine did when I had real hair. Holly really is a much better anti-depressant than the ones I'm taking.

The next five days involve teaching Holly increasingly complex hair styles from her book and listening in on long phone calls to Aunt Sophie about Mum's continuing health care once she's left the hospital. I listen for what seems like hours on end to phrases such as, "Uh uh," and "Right," and

"That makes sense," from Aunt Sophie. I worry about Mum's 'potential respiratory disorders' as I lie awake on the last full night of 2018. Mum told me that respiratory disorders are an umbrella term used to describe a variety of issues related to the heart and lungs. A whole load of questions fill my head:

What if these disorders are very serious?

What if she dies?

What if I never get to say goodbye?

What if she has a cardiac arrest or something all alone in her long term care facility?

I try to drag these thoughts from my mind as I drift off to sleep. However the questions creep back, manifesting themselves as a chain of nightmares. There's dream after dream about me entering Mum's room and her body being covered in scratchy hospital bed linen, where her life support machines are no longer switched on and beeping, no longer pumping oxygenated blood around her body. Every nightmare is more real and even more terrifying than the last. I gasp as I'm thrown back into petrified consciousness. My heart pumps adrenaline around my body as I curl up on my side praying that another nightmare won't come at me. But unfortunately, every time I close my eyes again, a similar variation of the same dream invades my sleep. Subsequently I'm actually glad to be woken up by Holly at quarter to seven demanding more stories about Holly The Mermaid and her magical family.

This time I tell a story about Holly The Mermaid using her supernatural healing powers to help an injured bottlenose dolphin. I reel on and on about the brave young mermaid's quest to find the magical pearl at the bottom of the ocean. *Pearl.* Even using her name in the context of the story hurts like mad. I fight through the pain but the story's plot gets weaker

the more I say her name and think about the horrendous crash
that took her, and my family, away from me.

When I've finished telling the story my cousin snuggles
down next to me in her Minnie Mouse pyjamas. Her warm,
curled up body beside me is like a bright beacon of hope and
strength in a dark forest.

Chapter 22

2019 is fast approaching and it feels like an impending misery coming my way. This will be the first New Year without my family. This will be the New Year without my best friend by my side and... OH MY GOD! At some point, probably in the next week, I'll have to go back to school. School was bad enough last summer term with the endless homework assignments, and that was before we'd even started the GCSE courses. Pearl always said 'School' should really stand for "**S**ociological **C**ruelty **H**eaped **O**n **O**ur **L**oved-Ones!"

The evening of December 31st creeps closer and closer. I don't want the New Year to come if it'll be as crappy as 2018 was. I don't want to lose anyone else that I love. I don't want to struggle through a year where there's a similar amount of tough twists and turns.

Holly is now running around in her pyjamas shouting,

"I get to stay up late tonight," over and over again. "For the first time, I get to stay up till midnight!" she squeals, showing off her gappy teeth.

"Yes my angel," says Aunty Rose, "It's very exciting isn't it."

Jack starts having one of his tantrums. I feel sure he doesn't understand the concept of New Year but he gets the idea of staying up late.

"I don't want to go to bed now. I want to stay up really late like Holly and Ocean."

Holly then pulls a face at Jack and they start having a full on fisty cuffs argument. Aunty Rose and Aunt Sophie have to physically separate them from each other.

"Stop it," yells Aunt Sophie, suddenly becoming her assertive lawyer self, "Or you will also be going to bed early Holly!" That prevents Holly from pulling her younger brother's hair out.

Once Jack's tucked up and Aunty Rose, Aunt Sophie and I have read him a story each, Jack finally snuggles down to sleep with his grey shark teddy tucked under his chin. I quietly close the *Tiger Who Came To Tea* and silently exit his room. I'm getting more skilful with these crutches every day.

When I hop back into the lounge Holly is already slumped on the sofa with her eyes almost closing.

"I'm not tired," she keeps insisting through loud, sleepy yawns. "I'm a big girl. I can stay awake."

That's the last we hear from Holly before she's fast asleep, despite it only being quarter to nine. Aunty Rose scoops her up and slowly carries Holly into her pink, dinosaur bedroom. When she comes back into the lounge she shuts the door behind her and then says,

"Party time."

She walks over to the drinks cabinet and takes out a bottle of vodka.

"Can I have one?" I ask, thinking the reply will almost one hundred percent be "No way you're only fourteen!"

But Aunty Rose nods,

"Yeah of course you can. I think you deserve a bit of fun Ocean after what you've been through in the last six months." Aunty Rose pours me a shot glass of vodka and adds some ice. The bitter taste burns the back of my throat.

Aunty Rose and Aunt Sophie put on Jools Holland. I furtively pour myself another shot from the bottle. It may be horrible tasting but I'm feeling all warm and airy.

I spend the next hour watching new and emerging musicians on the TV. Some of them seem very talented, but it's difficult to tell because my head is getting increasingly confused. I know I shouldn't, but because my Aunties are focussed on the TV and having some downtime from Holly and Jack, I keep topping up my shot glass. It feels so fun. By the time it's five minutes to midnight my brain feels all whizzy and wonderful. As the countdown to 2019 draws closer and closer all I can do is loudly giggle.

"Ten, nine," the countdown has started.

"Eight, seven, six…"

We join in

"Five four,"

Not long now

"Three two one….HAPPY NEW YEAR!!"

We all shout as we hug each other and the fireworks start going off outside.

Suddenly my head starts to spin and I feel really sick.

"You okay there Ocean?" asks Aunt Sophie, unaware (as yet) of the half empty bottle on the table

"I think I'm gonna go to bed," I say, "My head…" But before I can finish my sentence I full-on chunder all over the living room floor.

"Oh my goodness" says Aunty Rose, realising as she picks up the vodka bottle how much I've had.

"I only meant for you to have a little bit."

I feel so woozy and start to mumble

"Sorry…"

"Let's get you into bed Ocean" says Aunt Sophie, but she has a smile on her face.

Chapter 23

I wake up the next morning and my head feels like cotton wool. Every cell in my body is crying out. I'm still wearing my attire from last night. My wig is still stuck on and my eyes feel all crunchy from the mascara that was never washed off. I can't get my tongue off the roof of my mouth. It appears to be stuck there. I feel so thirsty. I reach over and pick up the glass of water that's on my bedside table. I take a small sip and I wonder if I'm going to be sick again.

What will they think of me?

Am I turning into a drug addict?

You hear stories.

I drift into and out of sleep for the next couple of hours. When I eventually get out of bed my right leg doesn't feel like it can take my body weight. I feel as though I've forgotten how to use my crutches. The water in the shower feels warm and kind, like a gentle pat from an old friend. Once I've taken my makeup off from last night I get into some washing-powder-scented pyjamas. I then clean my teeth and the minty taste is a nice replacement to the flavour of stale sick. Despite that my head still throbs behind my eyes, I'm starting to feel slightly more human. I decide to vacate my room, as lying back down would completely defeat the point of my shower.

I'm met by Aunty Rose who looks a lot more awake than I feel. Memories of last night start flooding back. Being carried back to my room by both Aunty Rose and Aunt Sophie. I remember Aunty Rose deciding to sleep in the armchair in my room.

"I just want to make sure nothing bad will happen to her," I think I remember her saying.

"I'm sorry," I croak.

Aunty Rose gives me a smile.

"That's okay," she says. "How's your head?"

"It feels like I've legit got a chainsaw being stabbed through my brain."

Aunty Rose laughs, showing off her straight, pearly white teeth; suggesting that she strongly remembers the first New Year that *she* got as drunk as I was last night.

"You look pretty rough," she says softly. "We had no idea you were topping up your glass all evening. Vodka's pretty strong stuff isn't it?"

She chuckles and I nod despondently.

"Why don't you go and lie on the sofa. I'll make you some tea and then go and change your sheets, you were quite sick last night."

I think I'm experiencing my first hangover!

The sofa and the fluffy blankets and cushions feel soft and enveloping as I snuggle down into the squidgy upholstery. Aunty Rose comes in five minutes later with a huge mug of milky tea and two pieces of toast with heart attack inducing amounts of golden butter.

"I always found this was a good hangover cure," she says as she puts the tray down beside the sofa.

"Once you've eaten, I'll get some paracetamol. Then you can go back to bed. Sophie's taken Holly and Jack to the park so you could have a lie in. I don't think they'll be back for some time yet."

I gently sip my tea and nibble at my toast. Although every mouthful is a struggle, Aunty Rose has words of wisdom.

"You'll feel a lot better once you've got these calories down you and then had a nap."

And she's right. After I've had a long sleep in my freshly made bed, which smells of tumble-dried sheets and homeliness, I do feel quite a bit better. I'm beginning to think my Aunties are quite amazing!

Chapter 24

Over the next few days I feel better and better. That is until the dreadful day comes when I have to start thinking about the start of the school term. The day before I'm due to return Aunt Sophie sits down with me on the sofa.

"So Ocean," she says slowly, "I think now would be a good time to talk about going back to your old house to grab some things."

It's at this point I realise I haven't actually thought much about most of my old stuff since I moved in here.

"Yes," I say finally. "I probably should... get my school uniform."

I know that my skirt won't look right now, so I'll have to wear my pair of school trousers and I have a few paint brushes and other things I feel I need. I now realise that I've seriously missed Cooky (my teddy bear). I picture him still sprawled on my bed, wanting to know where I've gone. Thank God I decided not to take him on holiday with me. If I had, he'd be dead like Dad and Pearl. I've missed running my hands over his soft brown fur and looking into his black beady eyes.

It feels strange pulling up outside my old house. I am immediately haunted by memories of Pearl at every age. She runs up to the front door and walks up the street to the park, with her nose stuck in a book.

The house looks almost the same way it did on the fateful day I left with my family for a holiday which was supposed to be amazing. However, the front garden looks more wild and overgrown and there's a 'For Sale' sign outside. I gawp and give Aunt Sophie a questioning look.

"We're having to sell it," she explains. "I'm sorry. It's the only way we can afford your mum's care and you'll get some of the money too."

Anger fizzes up inside me.

"Why didn't you ask me first? How dare you sell it, how dare you?"

"As I said," says Aunt Sophie in a soft voice, "We have to sell it so your mum can get the proper care she needs. The estate agent is coming tomorrow for showings, so it's your last chance to get anything you need."

"You should have asked me before you went and put my childhood home on the market!" I shout, feeling my body temperature rising with the anger.

"You couldn't have lived there could you?" says Aunt Sophie. "The bathroom isn't accessible, at least where you live now has an accessible room and everything's one floor."

I think about when Grandad John was ill and only had a couple of months to live, he moved in with my aunties and cousins. As a result of this there is a chair in the shower room so that I can sit down whenever I'm in there.

I guess she's right.

Aunt Sophie opens the door to the house. The slight creak it once made has turned into a menagerie of mice, all whining and squeaking for attention. There's the same cream carpet in the living room, it's soft and snug under foot. The multi bag of crisps still sits on the side, the very same multibag that Dad took packets out of last summer. The cushions look the same as they did on the day we left forever.

When I eventually get up to the bedroom that Pearl and I shared, I feel tears brimming in my eyes. I blink them back fast, I don't want Aunt Sophie to think I'm weak. The bedroom is frozen in time, it looks the exact same way it looked on the day that I left, completely oblivious of the fateful events about to take place. Pearl's bed is still neatly made, with her pillow perfectly plumped and her eiderdown carefully pulled across. My bed completely juxterposes my twin's. The pillow is still on the floor like it was when we had our pillow fight and the eiderdown is in a messy heap.

I sit on the bed and untangle Cooky from his linen prison. I know that I'm almost fifteen but sometimes the thing you most crave is a hug from a soft toy. I hold him close to my chest. I wish that Pearl hadn't decided to take Bumble with her. If she hadn't I'd still be able to hold something that she'd once loved. I sit there for a moment letting the tears run down my face.

I no longer care what Aunt Sophie thinks.

Eventually I get up and find my art supplies and put them in a bag. Although I have lots of new supplies from Christmas I don't think that you can have too many.

I find my school uniform stuffed in the back of my wardrobe with that 'it's the end of the summer term' crumpled appearance. I know that my school trousers need to be shortened on one leg and then hemmed. I know that I'll be working late into the evening to get them looking respectable.

"Is there anything else that you want?" asks Aunt Sophie.

"No," I say.

Aunty Rose already got most of my clothes before I came home so I don't think there's really anything else.

Looking around I see Pearl everywhere. I see her in the framed poems on the wall, her careful handwriting giving doors into the worlds she imagined so beautifully. One phrase catches my eye. '*And I know the sun will come out tomorrow*'

Will it?

Can it ever?

I take the poem from the wall and hug it close to me. Then I feel Aunt Sophie's arms around me and the tears flow freely.

After a while we head down stairs and I shut the door behind me for the very last time.

★ ★ ★

"How did it go?" asks Aunty Rose later that evening. "It must have been hard for you Ocean?"

I nod but keep my mouth shut. I don't want another Touchy Feely conversation right now. For the next twenty minutes I sit blankly on the sofa as Aunty Rose and Aunt Sophie discuss things like '*trusts*' and '*care home funding*' and '*her future*'. I don't care about any of that at the moment. Pearl should have been there with me today. She should have picked up her stuff and cried about leaving our house together with me. *I can't do this alone.* She should have put her arm around me and said

"Come on Oceay, let's go."

She should have hugged me tight on the way back. Instead I just sat in the front of the car and hugged myself. I didn't want Aunt Sophie to notice so whenever she glanced over to me my arms would be back by my sides.

After I've hemmed my trousers but before I go to bed, I use all of my art supplies, including the ones I collected today, to paint what the old house felt like without my family there.

I draw the house shrouded in shadow, with poison ivy growing wild and without care. I make sure that there are no bright colours. I make the actual exterior of the house look cracked and close to collapsing, with the odd brick missing here and there. Beside the house I paint a pile of burning rubble, covered by angry yellow, orange and red; the colours of the flames which stole my family. Smoke billows from the heap of rubbish, made up of everything that kept our family together.

It's so easy to not appreciate the small things, the seemingly inconsequential things which held us together. Things such as: making cakes with Dad, or Mum helping me with my science homework or going swimming with Pearl. Before the accident I never realised these things. I suppose it's because I always thought that they'd be around forever. I'd do anything now to taste Dad's famous chocolate cake or have Mum correct me or have swimming races with Pearl at the leisure centre. I draw translucent, ghostly figures floating around the house, completely disconnected from their earthly life.

Finally I put my paint brush down and decide to go to bed. When I'm lying in the world of soft duvets with Cooky by my side I hear Pearl's voice saying,

"That's an excellent picture. You're so talented."

"Thank you," I whisper into the darkness.

Chapter 25

The next morning arrives like a tropical rain storm, quickly and with little warning. When my alarm goes off at half past six I groan, my head still buried under the duvet. I still haven't got the same morning bounce I once had. My school uniform feels completely weird now. The pair of trousers cut shorter on one leg just looks tragic and wrong. My tie feels tight around my neck and my stomach protrudes far, far more than it once did. I stare at my burn scarring in the mirror and wonder if anyone could possibly recognise me.

My phone is pinging like mad.

Hafsa: Can't believe your gonna b in school

Madeline: Can't wait to see you at break

Hafsa: It'll by fine hun

Madeline: See you laturrr x

And so on. Wish I shared their enthusiasm.

After we drop Holly and Jack at their primary school, it takes about ten minutes to drive to mine. Having left primary more than three years ago, I've forgotten the hassle involved with dropping kids off, such as Aunt Sophie having neglected to sign their reading records during the holidays, and the general fuss as Jack falls over his new shoes, and the palaver of signing them into their classes. Finally Aunt Sophie reappears and we head off.

The gates of Hillbrook Secondary School seem far more oppressive than they've ever appeared, even more so than on my first day of year seven. As I hop into my form class, which luckily has always been on the ground flour, I feel like everyone is staring at me. I enter the classroom and Ms Hennison, who I've always thought hated me more than anyone else in the entire school, approaches me.

"Hi there Ocean," she says in a silky sweet tone, which I didn't know her voice was capable of.

"How are you feeling?"

"Clearly I'm doing just great," I say sarcastically through gritted teeth.

I think Ms Hennison will scream at me at this point. I want her to. But of course she doesn't.

I've now got Sick-Kid-Status.

I don't want her to be nice to me just because I'm now disabled. She points to my desk I had in year nine, right next to Madeline. There's an empty seat where Pearl once sat. I flash back to her informative contributions to the group; contributions that she won't be able to make again. *Oh God, this is so frickin' weird.*

Madeline smiles at me.

"Hi Ocean," she says, in a voice which isn't quite her happy go lucky self.

She looks exactly the same as she did nearly 6 months ago. Long black curly hair and big almond eyes.

"Hey," I reply. "How've you been? Thanks for your messages, means a lot."

"Okay," Madeline replies, looking down. "I've missed you and…"

"Pearl?" I finish for her.

I can tell this is going to be difficult.

"I'm so sorry that you ended up like this," says Madeline.

I shrug. "I'm not gonna lie, it is pretty shit but… but the rest of my family had it far worse obviously."

Madeline looks down, a tear visible on her cheek.

"How do you cope?" she asks. "I can't imagine losing Hannah like that."

I'm about to answer that I don't cope at all. My depression is so bad. But Ms Hennison starts to take the register.

"Madeline?" she calls out.

"Yes Miss," says Madeline.

"Asad?"

"Yes Miss," says Asad.

Everyone sits open-mouthed when my name is called out and I answer

"Yes Miss."

I hear Jody Summers whispering to Amber Smith.

"I thought she was like dead or something."

Pearl and I used to hang out with Jody and Amber. That was before they told everyone I had a crush on Joel. Jody was eavesdropping from the bench next to mine and Pearl's. She's the reason why I only have two friends now: Hafsa and Madeline. Although, having said that, they are very good friends to have. They're the kind of friends who always know exactly what to get you for your birthday. I think about my birthday coming up in just a few weeks - the first birthday without Pearl.

How will I bear it?

I receive more open gasps and hear more whispers of '*Oh my god it's that Ocean girl*' as I go to the first period which is art. I excitedly enter the classroom. I'm greeted by Ms Williams, her blue eyes twinkling with the same wonder as the last time I was in her class.

"Ocean!" she says excitedly, "I've missed you so much in my lessons!"

"Hi Miss," I say in breathless delight, "I've missed your art classes as well."

Her wrinkled face beams. She looks just the same, same smile in her eyes, the same short grey hair and the same scar on her forehead. I often wonder how she got it.

I've been thinking a lot more often about scars recently.

I'm lucky because in art class they are starting a new topic so I can pretty much just jump into my coursework. We're looking at self portraits. Ms Williams shows us an example up on the board. It's her own self portrait.

"Here's one I made earlier," she says proudly. I gaze up in wide eyed wonder at her painting. Every brush stroke is in the perfect place. Her short grey curly hair a perfect replica of the real thing, down to every last bouncy ringlet. Ms Williams has even drawn the viewer's eye to the scar that spans the width of her hair line. I think this is exceptionally brave of her because it must cause her so much anxiety.

She's not frightened of who she is.

This makes me decide to draw myself the way I am now. I draw every last millimeter of damaged skin; making sure I don't miss any of it out. I don't hesitate to draw my body without a left leg. I draw myself clutching my crutches, because again, this is now the difficult reality of my new physical appearance. I hesitate as I'm about to start sketching the outline of my wig. *Should I?* I wonder to myself. If I did it would make me seem as what I appear. But on the other hand, I don't actually have any hair now. In the end I decide to add it. It feels like part of me now.

"Be true to who you are!" says Ms Williams. "Don't add anything that doesn't feel true to how you really feel."

She's such a great teacher.

* * *

"So how did it go?" asks Aunty Rose that afternoon, when she picks me up from school.

I shrug.

"It was actually okay, you know. Like Maths, English and Physics were… they were pretty crappy. But art, which we had first, was good."

"What did you do?" asks Aunty Rose, as she gently turns the steering wheel, knowing cars still make me nervous.

"Self portraits," I answer.

"That sounds interesting," says Aunty Rose. "But was it hard for you?" she asks.

"No, not really," I reply, looking out the window, "Because I just drew what was real." When we get back, Holly is very excited to tell me all about PE at school.

"So Olivia and me ran and we got the ball in the goal and… you're not listening are you Ocean?"

I realise that I'm so tired from my day at school that my eyes are nearly closed.

"No, I am." I yawn, pushing myself up to a sitting position on the sofa. "You were saying, you and Anna…"

"Olivia!!!" corrects Holly.

"Sorry," I say, shaking my head, "You and Olivia."

"Yes," says Holly, "We scored a goal in PE and the boys in my class were really mean and said that girls can't play football. But they can can't they Ocean?"

I nod.

"Yes, of course they can." I decide that, after I've done my school work, I will try and find some women's football clips to show Holly. It'll give her a confidence boost.

For dinner that night we have pizza. I'm shocked that two slices each seem to completely fill up Jack and Holly. I mean, of course, Pearl and I ate less as little kids but I don't remember ever eating as small a portion as that. I power through five slices of pizza no bother and feel like maybe I could have eaten more.

"You must be knackered," says Aunt Sophie, watching me rub my eyes and yawning. "Why don't you have an early night tonight?"

Normally I'd refuse and say "No I'm fine honestly." But my eyes feel as heavy as lead, so I yawn and say,

"Okay."

I lie in bed and reflect on my day at school. It was a mixture. Some people treated me with too much kindness and spoke to me in patronising tones, but others like Jodie Summers whispered behind my back. Is this what it's like having a disability? I never realised how different people are treated when they look or act differently to everyone else. At least Ms Williams understood me in the art class. She's such a star. I guess the day could have gone far, far worse.

Chapter 26

The next few weeks roll on by at school. People are the same amount of over-the-top-nice to me or behind-my-back-whispery. One time I hear the teachers talking in hushed voices as I pass the staff room.

"Poor Ocean Rodrigo!"

"Apparently her Mum may never wake up."

"She hasn't really got a Mum anymore."

These kind of words make my blood boil. Just because she can't hold a conversation any more, because she's drifting in and out of consciousness, it doesn't mean she's not my Mum. Although her heart is damaged, it still beats for Pearl and Dad and me. I know for sure I'm right.

One Friday lunchtime I sit in the library with Hafsa and Madeline. The snow blowing on the playground looks too cold, especially for me now that I can't move around as much without getting really tired.

"It's so nice that you're back in school," says Hafsa. "We were all told you'd been in an accident. We weren't sure quite how bad it was. But the fact that you weren't coming back for week after week made me very worried."

"And we were all so shocked about Pearl...and..." says Madeline.

"Yeah," I say, trying to act matter of fact about it but struggling, "I miss my Dad too."

There's an awkward pause until I steal a chip from Hafsa's plate and she steals a crisp from my lunch box. The four of us, Pearl, Hafsa, Madeline and I used to share bits and pieces from each other's plates and lunch boxes. I remember Pearl sharing her giant chocolate cookie between the four of us, pedantically checking that all the quarters were exactly the same size. I wince at the memory of my sister. Everything about her is becoming increasingly vague with every day that passes.

When I was first told that Pearl and Dad had died in the crash it was like a highlighter had been drawn round every memory I had of them. But now, that highlighter is being rubbed out more and more, it seems with every passing hour. How would Pearl feel if she knew I was beginning to forget things about her?

No, not forget. Just not quite remember. I want to always remember - every detail.

That evening I collapse on the sofa, as I do most days after I return from the prison that is school. I watch as Holly and Jack get their hats, gloves, scarves and coats on to go for a snowball fight outside with Aunty Rose. Aunt Sophie sits on a chair near the sofa and smiles at me.

"So Ocean," she begins, "It's your birthday next Saturday, and we haven't discussed what you're going to do."

I shake my head.

"I don't want to do anything."

Aunt Sophie gives me a sympathetic look.

"I understand," she says, "But I'm sure Pearl would not want you missing out on your special day."

She pauses.

"In fact, I'm sure she'd agree with me when I say that you deserve a good birthday. Last year was so difficult for you, we all know that."

She catches her breath.

"When I first got the call from the hospital they said that... they said that you most likely weren't going to survive the night, that's how bad your injuries were. I wanted to come and sit with you, you know be there to hold your hand. But they didn't let me at first."

I had no idea before this point how ill I was after the car crash. How close to death I'd been. Would that have been better? At least I'd be with Pearl now doing whatever ghost twins do.

"So," says Aunt Sophie, pulling herself together, "What do you want to do?"

I think for a second.

"I'm thinking keep it relatively chill," I say. "Pizza, film and a couple of friends?"

Aunt Sophie stands up quickly from her chair.

"I'll go and get a piece of paper and pen to plan."

"It's just a film night," I call after her. "Not a bloody dinner party."

Despite my comments, Aunt Sophie is determined to plan my fifteenth birthday party down to a tee. We decide the kind of pizza: margherita, because it's what both my friends like, friends: obviously Hafsa and Madeline and the film: *Pitch Perfect*.

"It's a modern classic," I assure Aunt Sophie when she presents me with a puzzled look. Aunt Sophie even wants to plan the movie snacks. We start listing: popcorn / pringle crisps / chocolate... But then Holly and Jack come back in from the snow. They're cold and hungry so Aunt Sophie has to start making them dinner and give Holly therapy about her lonely snowman.

"I don't want him to be sad!" she cries. "Why can't I bring him inside so that he can have friends?"

After ten minutes, Aunty Rose says, with a tired sigh. "I'll tell you what. I'll go and make your snowman a friend. Okay?"

Holly nods. "But won't they both be really cold? It's freezing outside!"

* * *

That weekend Aunt Sophie and I do even more birthday planning. I'm reminded of the plans Pearl and I made last year. We went bowling with Hafsa and Madeline at the local leisure centre. We then went for burgers and chips at the cafe. Madeline laughed so much that strawberry milkshake shot out of her nose, which only made us all laugh even more. This year would be a more solemn occasion because I'm not sharing it with Pearl as I have ever since the day we were both born. The hug at the doorway when they arrive will feel somewhat empty. *Pitch Perfect* won't be as funny as the last time I saw it with Pearl. The pizza won't taste right.

However, it's very kind of my aunties to be throwing me this party seeing as they've already got two kids' birthdays to worry about.

I send a text to the new group chat I've formed with Hafsa and Madeline since getting my new phone.

Hey. You guys free next Saturday for pizza and movie night?

Madeline is the first to reply.

Sounds gr8. What's the address?

Then Hafsa sends a text.

Sounds amazing. Can't wait. What do you want for your Bday?

I look up at Aunt Sophie with the beginnings of a smile

"Yes," I say, "They can both come."

The next week at school seems to fly by like an agile bird gliding through the sky. I love having something to look forward to. Madeline and Hafsa start winking at each other when we sit in the library. I think they're discussing presents. The two of them always seem to get such special gifts. Like for our twelfth birthday Hafsa got us each some fluffy socks and a hot chocolate set, with mini marshmallows and everything, and Madeline got us some nice smelling bubble bath. They're two of the most generous people I know. As we say goodbye at the gates on Friday, Hafsa says:

"Enjoy your birthday until we see you tomorrow."

I'm going to try really hard to enjoy our get together even though I miss Pearl so much.

Chapter 27

Holly and Jack bounce into my room at quarter to eight the next morning, which is actually pretty late for them.

"Happy Birthday Ocean!" squeals Holly, bouncing up and down, her hair flying out behind her.

"We got you presents," says Jack excitedly.

"Open mine first," says Holly. "It's some more pastels for your art."

I smile at my naive younger cousins, who clearly haven't yet grasped the concept of a surprise.

"I've got you a mug," says Jack.

I still act completely surprised when I tear off the wrapping paper and give them both a big hug.

"You two are the best," I say.

"I'm the bestest though aren't I?" says Holly

"No, I am" says Jack.

I solve the argument by tickling them both until they are laughing hysterically.

Aunt Sophie has made me a special breakfast of homemade croissants and strawberry jam.

"This is my favourite breakfast," I say. "Thank you so much."

Despite the happy occasion, there's something missing and that something, or rather someone, is obviously Pearl. Pearl should be here with me now, getting a food baby from eating so much puff pastry. Pearl should be opening her gifts with me. We should be blowing out the candles of the chocolate cake on the kitchen side together. The day doesn't feel right.

Aunty Rose and Aunt Sophie give me a voucher for Next.

"Let's go on a shopping spree!" says Aunt Sophie. "We can get some stuff for your room. It'll make it feel even more like yours."

We drive into the town centre and park up. I haven't been into town since my accident and the busy bustling is very overwhelming. I can feel eyes on where the bottom part of my leg should be.

"Next is only across here," says Aunt Sophie gesturing to a road with two sets of traffic lights. It's a struggle to cross but Aunt Sophie finds somewhere for me to sit down for a minute.

We browse Next for ages. We smell every candle and inspect every duvet and pillowcase set. We leave Next with a blue spotty double duvet set, two matching pillow cases and a lavender candle.

"I love the smell of it and all," I begin, "But a candle… it's still fire." Aunt Sophie gives me a sympathetic look.

"I promise you, Ocean, it'll be fine. Okay?"

I nod

"Okay," I say.

"And now," says Aunt Sophie, "The ice cream shop." She points at a shop on the opposite side of the road to Next called Creamy Ice Creams.

"They could have thought of a slightly more imaginative name," says Aunt Sophie, just before we go in.

Creamy Ice Creams has the biggest range of ice creams you'll ever see in your life. They have all the classics of course, chocolate, strawberry, vanilla, but they also have a whole load of exotic flavours like Lemon Dream, Chilli Chocolate and Cheeky Frog. Cheeky Frog is apparently made from 'all natural ingredients' but the neon green colour would suggest otherwise! Pearl always had the bubblegum flavour and would end up with blue ice cream all round her lips. Eventually I choose Cookie Dough ice cream in a cone, because it's one of my all time faves.

* * *

Hafsa and Madeline arrive at the same time that evening.

"Happy birthday!" they both say, huge grins on their faces as they both pass me presents.

"Oh my God!" I half yell, "Thank you so much!" I'm so pleased to see them.

Aunty Rose and Aunt Sophie welcome them into the sitting room, where the pizzas and snacks are already laid out on the big coffee table.

Madeline has got me some perfume that smells of citrus. I realise from the Chanel label that it's *quality*.

"Thank you so much," I say, giving my friend a big bear hug.

Hafsa has got me a collection of sustainable lip balms.

"It's the thing now," she says. "Sustainability. You know, the school strikes around the world because of Greta Thunberg? These are made from parts of fruits which normally go to waste."

I gently sniff the cherry scented one. It smells more like actual fruit than any other lip balm I've had before.

"That's awesome!!!" I say. "Thank you so much." Tears of half-joy, half-sadness at Pearl not being here to share in this moment, start to gather in my eyes, making my mascara smudge. *But no. My friends have come for a nice evening and I should really pull myself together.*

I enjoy watching *Pitch Perfect* with my two best friends. We all laugh hysterically at all the same points, like when Aubrey is sick all over the auditorium and they start throwing vomit at each other. We eat so much pizza and junk food that by the end of the movie we struggle to get up.

"I love that film so much" says Madeline "It's just like, so feel-good."

"True Dat" I say. "And so many great songs."

We start singing the medley from the end of the movie, our voices getting more wild with every line. Within a couple of minutes we can't sing a note in tune because we're laughing so much.

"*Yeahhhhhh. It's a party in the the USA,*" belts Hafsa, wiggling her shoulders.

Madeline picks up a breadstick as a microphone and raps one of the songs from the RiffOff.

"*It's going down, fade to Blackstreet. The homies got at me, collab' creations, bump like acne...*"

"You got this!" I'm cheering.

"I know right. School's a waste of time with talents like mine," shouts Madeline.

"Not" adds Hafsa.

"Maybe keep the day job for now?" I suggest.

All three of us dissolve into giggles yet again.

Too soon it's time for my friends to leave.

"Thank you so much for the great party," says Madeline, "It was so fun."

"Yes," says Hafsa, "It was bangin'." Hafsa's mum rolls her eyes and thanks Aunt Sophie. After a few more hugs and blown kisses they're gone.

That night as I lie in bed, with my new duvet cover, I wonder what we'd have done if Pearl were still allive and we'd never gotten in that stupid car for the stupid holiday. We might have gone ice skating or to Thorpe Park or one of those high-rope adventure days.

It was a good birthday Pearl.

As I'm drifting off to sleep I think I hear her whisper.

Happy Birthday Oceay.

Chapter 28

The next morning, Jack decides that he wants to go to the park on his scooter.

"I never go on it," he whines.

Aunt Sophie looks up from her computer.

"I know darling but me and Mummy are both working today." She looks stressfully back down at the legal document she's reading. I don't know why she works from home with two young kids, she never gets all that much done and ends up having to read documents late into the night to make up for it.

"I know," I say to Holly and Jack. "Why don't we go and build a den in my room? I've got loads of extra cushions and blankets in my cupboard."

"A den?" says Jack excitedly. "Can we live in it forever and ever?"

"Come on," I say, nodding towards my room. Holly and Jack, with my instructions, actually build an okay den. It keeps falling down to begin with, but the hours spent den building with Pearl in our living room means I know how to fix all issues relating to their construction.

"Can I go and get my bears?" asks Jack, already running in the direction of his bedroom.

Before long there's no way I can use my crutches to get out of my room because there are piles of teddies, bunnies and an assortment of other soft animals strewn over the floor, as well as Jack's Teddy Bear Picnic Set. I recognise it as being the one that Pearl and I used to play with when we were little.

* * *

The next day at school starts like any other. I meet Hafsa and Madeline just outside the school gates, where I'm dropped every morning. They walk slowly, so as not to overtake me and my crutches. We enter our form class and go our separate ways for our individual lessons. It's at morning break where things are different. Hafsa and Madeline go to the canteen and I sit on one of the benches in the year ten playground. Jodie comes up to me and hisses in my ear.

"Hey Chicken Skin."

She then slopes off to stand with her gaggle of 'popular' friends. The words sting because they're true. I do have 'chicken skin'. I don't have the same exterior as I once did.

Hafsa and Madeline return two minutes later.

"I bought you something," says Madeline, passing me a giant chocolate chip cookie.

"Thank you." I pat the space on the bench next to me and they both sit down.

"That was such a great party at the weekend," says Hafsa. "Your aunties have a really nice house."

"Thank you." I smile taughtly, not wanting them to know what's just been said to me.

At lunch time, when Hafsa and Madeline go to the loo, Jodie comes up to me and looks me deep in the eyes.

"You're very ugly aren't you, Ocean?" She then slinks off again, to her lair of nasty friends. Like at break time I pretend that nothing is wrong to Hafsa and Madeline. They don't seem to notice that anything's up. I think this is good. Madeline with her temper might go up and punch Jodie. Before my accident, if something like that had been said to Pearl, Hafsa or Madeline that's what I would have done. There's no way that any one would have tried to cross me. They knew what was headed for them if they did.

That evening, to enable Aunt Sophie to finish her work, and before Aunty Rose gets back from the hospital, I listen to Jack read.

"The magg... the magg..." he stutters, as he squints at the Biff and Chip book on the table.

"Magic," I correct. "Keep going though. You're doing really well."

These words make him beam. I then help Holly with her four times tables, which she's been set as homework. I miss the days when there was so little work to do after school. I look at my long list of assignments due tomorrow: Chemistry, English, German and RE. It doesn't help that I have no clue what's going on in most of my lessons, due to the amount of time I've missed.

I read Jack *The Tiger Who Came To Tea* and read Holly the first chapter of *Lily Alone* by Jaqueline Wilson.

"Another chapter!" pleads Holly.

"No, no," I say, putting a book mark inside the book before closing it.

"Cliff hanger. I'll read you another chapter tomorrow." She nods and curls up into a tight ball.

When I get back into the kitchen, Aunty Rose is back from work. She's sprawled on the sofa with big dark circles under her eyes. Her eyes also look red, like she's been crying.

"Was your day okay?" I ask slowly.

"Exhausting," says Aunty Rose. "There was a car crash. A brother and sister were brought to us. It reminded me of... your accident."

I don't know what to say.

"Thank you for putting the kids to bed," says Aunt Sophie, clearly trying to change the subject to one that doesn't make her, Aunty Rose or me feel sad.

"We really appreciate it, especially with the amount of homework you must have."

For the next three hours I struggle through atomic structures, analyse *Walking Away* by Cecil Day Lewis, learn German vocabulary and do 'Buddhist beliefs' revision for a test I'm sure to fail. I always start the term with the best intentions (getting my homework done on the night that it's set / packing my books for the next day the night before and all that stuff) but by about halfway through the second week, these habits have fallen down a deep, dark drain. By eleven thirty I decide enough is enough. I close the RE textbook and get into bed.

Chapter 29

"Ocean?" asks Holly at breakfast the next morning, "What do you want to do once you're older?"

"Art," I say wistfully, looking down at my bowl of cornflakes that I'm spiralling around like a milky whirlpool.

"I want to be a doctor," says Holly proudly.

"I think you'd make a great doctor," says Aunt Sophie as she does up her coat, "But you won't be a good doctor if you're late for school. Come on." She picks up the car keys and starts to walk towards the front door.

It takes another ten minutes before my cousins are actually ready to go. Holly attempts to french plait her hair while I'm tying my right shoe laces. She's getting quite good at styling but it takes an age.

"Can you finish it Ocean?" she says.

"I don't have time," I huff, "I'll just do you a high pony, these are really cool too."

Holly sticks out her bottom lip at her reflection in the full length mirror. She shouts childish insults like "You're really mean," and "I thought we were friends," all the way to her school.

"What was all that about?" asks Aunt Sophie, as she drives away from the gates after the drop-off.

"I don't really know," I say looking out of the windows. "Just kids stuff I think."

Aunt Sophie nods. I can tell she's excited to go back into her solicitors office for the first time in a while. She drops me off outside the school gates again and Hafsa and Madeline walk alongside me to our form room. Again at break, when I'm alone on the bench, Jodie comes up to me, the same menacing look on her face.

"Chicken Skin," she hisses in my ear. "I can't believe anyone still loves you with skin like that. You're so ugly, Chicken Skin." And then she does something completely unexpected. She punches me in the arm.

She then says,

"That's just for starters Chicken Skin."

It hurts like hell, especially as she's punched my left arm which still hurts sometimes. But I sniff back the tears when Madeline and Hafsa come over.

"You okay?" asks Hafsa, as she takes a big bite of an apple.

"Yeah," I lie, resisting the urge to hold my throbbing arm.

"Have you seen this?" asks Madeline, showing me a meme on Instagram. I shake my head and force a laugh. They can't know what's been happening to me.

In English, the lesson before lunch, I can't focus on *Mother Any Distance* by Simon Armitage because I can't stop thinking about what Jodie said.

That's just for starters, Chicken Skin.

I wonder what horrendous thing she may have in store for me next.

Inevitably I find out just half an hour later. When Hafsa and Madeline go to their lockers, to get their PE kits, Jodie and Amber approach me.

"What are *you* doing?" sneers Amber. "I think she thinks she's special or something."

"Yeah," smirks Jodie. "Now she's got special needs. Or something."

"Hey Chicken Skin" says Amber, "Stand up."

I stay put.

"Stand up or I'll kill your Mum."

I oblige, although my Mum is now barely living. I'm about to give them a piece of my mind when Jodie shoves me to the ground. I stumble and fall hard against the bench, my ribs cracking off the edge of the seat. Oxygen is knocked from my lungs as a shooting pain grips my upper body.

"Now look what you've done? You're so stupid Chicken Skin."

"If you tell anyone," says Amber "We'll find your address and kill you in your sleep you stupid Chicken Skin." Her words are full of malice.

I want to fight back. I want to punch them in the face but all I can manage is to push myself back onto the bench. As I move I feel a crushing sensation in my chest. It feels like all the oxygen has been knocked out of me.

"This isn't over yet you know Chicken Skin," says Amber spitefully as they walk away.

Hafsa and Madaline walk over to the bench.

"You okay there Ocean?" asks Hafsa, "You don't look okay hun."

"Yeah, yeah I'm fine. It's just... period cramps." My two friends nod.

"Oh my God you poor thing," says Madeline, "They're like the worst thing ever."

"I mean there are worse things," I say bitterly, looking down at my stump.

"I'm so sorry." says Madeline in a fluster, "I know, that must be so much worse."

"Don't worry," I say sarcastically, "I mean, it'll grow back like my hair and my skin. It'll all be fine." With that I get up and hop over to a bench on the other side of the playground, my chest burning with pain. I narrowly miss getting hit by a basketball, my crutches clattering as I go, my rage intensifying.

I hear frantic footsteps behind me.

"We're sorry," calls out Hafsa. "We know it must be so difficult for you."

I spin around mid hop.

"No," I say, "You don't know what it's like. You never will and that's because you weren't in a car crash last year and you don't have debilitating injuries now as a result and you... you don't have to deal with feeling how I feel every time I look in the mirror and see this ugly wreck. My life is ruined. And I never want to see either of you ever again!" I scream and plonk myself down on the bench.

"What's all this about?" asks Madeline. "Has someone said something or...?"

"I'm warning you," I say, now seeing red everywhere I turn. "Get out of my sight. NOWWW!!!" I scream.

This makes my head of year Mr Hussein come over.

"What's going on here?" I notice the playground is suddenly very quiet. Everyone wants to know what the drama is.

"No... no ... nothing," I stutter.

"You seem very upset," he says sympathetically, "Why don't we go and find Ms Collins." Ms Collins is the other year head.

I stay put. I don't want anyone to know what's just happened. I just want to be left alone. I feel so alone.

"Come on Ocean," says Mr Hussein "I think Ms Collins has biscuits in her office and I know I could do with one". He's smiling kindly at me and I get up and start to hop towards the office. Gradually the playground comes back to life. As we approach the office the pain in my chest is extreme.

This really hurts.

"Are you okay Ocean?" asks Ms Collins offering me a custard cream. Mr Hussein has left us to resume patrolling the playground, complete with a couple of biscuits.

"You're obviously not okay" she adds. "Can you tell me about it?"

I'm shivering and trembling, waves pulsating down my chest.

"I don't know Miss," I mutter.

"I think perhaps I'd better call home," Ms Collins begins to say but suddenly I start to get vertigo. The room around me starts spinning like mad. I think I hear Ms Collins' concerned voice saying,

"You don't look well Ocean?"

My chest pain, which has been screaming for attention for the last twenty minutes, has now reached a whole new level of agony. I feel myself swaying uncontrollably side to side, like a rocky boat out at sea. And then I feel myself collapsing on the floor of Ms Collins' office.

Chapter 30

"Ocean? Ocean? Ocean?" I hear Aunt Sophie's worried voice somewhere nearby. My eyes flicker open.

"Take it slow now," says Aunt Sophie, "You're in hospital. Ocean you've got two broken ribs. How did it happen?"

Suddenly I feel like a small child again. Tears start rolling down my face.

"This girl Jodie," I manage through the tears, "She punched me earlier" I say. "I couldn't balance and I hit the bench really hard"

"Oh my God," says Aunt Sophie, "I'm going to have to call the school. This is serious." She walks off looking extremely stressed, still wearing her lawyer's suit.

"No," I can hear her saying just outside my curtains.

"No Ocean wouldn't lie. What do you mean you don't think Jodie would do something like that? Yes, that would be very helpful," she says.

At that moment a doctor comes and draws back my curtains.

"So," she says, "After speaking with some of my colleagues, we all agree it would be best to monitor you for the next twenty four hours. Is that okay?"

I nod. I want to do everything I can to stay away from the hell hole which is school. I know that Jodie will have it in for me if I go in before she's been expelled or whatever. The doctor then turns to Aunt Sophie.

"Does that sound alright?" she asks.

"I'm going to go home and get a couple things," says Aunt Sophie. "Will you be okay?"

I nod.

"I spent months in here by myself, I think I can handle an hour or two!" She smiles and walks off.

I look around the cubicle I'm in. It's not as big as the burns ward and there are only a couple of other patients lying around. I'm definitely the oldest here, by a mile. I see my phone on the bedside table. There's a message from Hafsa on the What's app group.

Ocean you OK? We saw you being taken away in an ambulance. What's wrong?

I send a reply.

Sorry for being such a bitch. Jodie's been at me for the last couple days when you guys are not with me. Today she punched me to the ground. Turns out I've got two broken ribs.

I look at the message. I can't believe it's the truth. You hear stories about people being physically and emotionally attacked for being different. But I never thought Jodie, cow though she is, would ever go quite that far.

I press send and a reply appears almost instantly from Madeline this time.

OMG! Does this mean you're off school for a bit? We'll miss you hun.

Although my chest hurts like mad and it's agony even to breathe in and out, it feels like a weight has been lifted off my shoulders by opening up to my friends.

When Aunt Sophie reappears with an overnight bag she looks very flustered.

"What is it?" I ask.

"Rose doesn't finish her shift until later this evening so it means that I've had to ask a neighbour to do dinner, bath and bed for Holly and Jack. They're going to miss you tonight Ocean."

I feel myself blush, something only Pearl did. Is my hard exterior beginning to crack? I never used to do tears, or breakdowns or any of that mushy stuff; well, not in front of most people anyway.

"No really," she says, "You're like…" she ponders, "A third Mum?"

She then looks me in the eye.

"You've been great with them ever since you moved in with us. It must be so difficult for you without Pearl."

I'm surprised to hear her say my sister's name.

The night is filled with beeping and nurses coming in to do my obs. I'd forgotten how patronisingly they say, "Alright sweetie I've come to do your blood-pressure."

Why can't they just talk to me like a fifteen year old?

By the following lunchtime, I'm being wheeled out to the car in a hospital wheelchair, because the pain in my chest is too bad to hop along. Aunt Sophie gently helps me to do a pivot transfer into the passenger seat of her car.

"I'm thinking," she says as she buckles her seatbelt in and turns on the engine, "You should stay off school until your chest is better. At least that horrible Jodie's been expelled."

"Expelled?" I'm genuinely surprised.

"Yes. Apparently she'd been on a final warning for her behaviour and that was the last straw. She tried to get her friends to lie for her but I think they were frightened when they realised what she'd done."

I think of Amber doing anything to get out of trouble, even dropping her supposedly best friend Jodie even though Amber was just as guilty.

I realise as we drive away, that this is the second time I've come out of the hospital car park in Aunt Sophie's car. She drives even more slowly and carefully than she usually does and says "Sorry Ocean," whenever she drives over speed bumps and hears me inhale sharply. When we get home, I go to my room and fall asleep for the next two hours.

"It's perfectly normal," says Aunty Rose later that evening, once she's back from working at the hospital I've just left.

"It's very normal for people with injuries like that to feel very tired for a few days after their accident."

That night, Aunty Rose and Aunt Sophie come in at regular intervals to give me painkillers.

For the next week, I pretty much just do all of my school work in my bed. I do my best but it's difficult to learn without proper input from the teachers. I try and muddle my way through quadratic equations, but none of it makes any sense. What I don't understand about GCSE maths is how can there be so much to learn about triangles. It's all Pythagorus and trigonometry and congruent shapes. Surely all that really needs to be learned is how to manage finance and how to know if you're being paid the correct amount? For the average person nothing else is required.

I wish my exams were cancelled next year. I run through all the possible things that could make this happen: nuclear war, natural disaster, a pandemic! Anything to mean I won't have to sit my GCSEs.

Gradually over the next week the pain becomes more bearable and I don't have to ask for as many painkillers. I'm

now able to sit on the sofa and continue reading *Lily Alone*
to Holly. She listens excitedly when Lily and her siblings leave
their flat and go to live in a local park. She gasps and looks
worried when Bliss falls out of their tree hideout and badly
breaks her leg. When I finish reading her the book, she agrees
with what Pearl and I thought when we read it: the ending is
the worst ending ever in the history of books.

"How can you end a book 'we are all going to be together
very, very soon' and then not write a sequel," ranted Pearl,
furiously shutting the book.

"What other books did you like when you were seven?" asks
Holly, looking up from trying to cut off the head of one of her
many teddies to be like Bliss's favourite teddy in *Lily Alone*.

"I'll have a think," I say, "But I think you should stop trying
to execute Mr Fluffy the Bear. I'm not sure he'd enjoy having
a head which half hangs off for the rest of his life. I mean, how
would you like it?"

Before Holly can stop herself there's a small snip sound as
my little cousin manages to cut about two centimeters into Mr
Fluffy's neck.

"OH NO!" wails Holly, "I've killed Mr Fluffy the Bear!"

"Pass him here," I say. "I think Mr Fluffy can be saved. I'll
sew him up for you later, but for now I think what Mr Fluffy
the Bear would really like, is for you to give him lots of hugs
and not come near him with the scissors ever again."

Holly sniffs back the tears and gives her fluffy, soft friend a
huge hug.

I have to take paracetamol and ibuprofen before the repair
on Mr Fluffy's neck. Holding my arms up when I'm sewing is
still very painful. I'm careful to make sure that I don't leave any

gaps in the bear's neck. Holly was in a state when she went to bed and treated us to an hour long crying fit.

"I'm worried he's in pain!" she cried, over and over again.

When I was a child I would have cried about similarly inconsequential stuff like that. My accident last summer, losing Dad, Pearl and Mum (in a way) and now having two broken ribs really puts the things that children get upset about into perspective. But *as* a child, losing your favourite blanket or breaking your favorite toy car, seems like the biggest issue ever. You can't understand why those around you aren't also weeping. I remember when we were four and my Granny Martha died, Mum cried for weeks on end. But when I lost my favourite hair scrunchy I couldn't understand why people weren't crying with me.

"TADAH!!!" I say the next morning at breakfast, as I reunite Holly with her friend.

"Oh wow!" says Aunty Rose, "What do we say to Ocean?"

"Thank you Ocean," says Holly with a smile. Mr Fluffy is squeezed so tight in her arms I'm worried my recent stitching will come undone!

"You're very welcome!" I coo back. "He's all better now. But I've also promised him that you'll be nicer to him in the future."

"I will. I promise." says Holly, looking down lovingly at the piece of stuffed fabric with a manufactured personality in her hand.

I'm still off school, doing the work from my bed. But with the help of my friend YouTube, I'm beginning to understand the concepts of compound interest. The highlight of my day is always reading stories to Holly and Jack, something I never thought I'd enjoy doing. Before my accident I wasn't much of a reader, but now the world of telling stories has opened up a bright new door... a door to a world which isn't as grey as the one that I'm living in.

Chapter 31

Being off school for long time-periods makes you feel like you're a ship lost at sea, which people have long stopped looking for. Although Jodie has now been expelled from school, the things that she said to me have stuck. The phrases 'You're so ugly' and the cruel nickname "Chicken Skin" physically hurt everytime I accidentally think about them. When I do think about all that stuff, the thoughts act like a giant whirlpool, sucking me in and not allowing me to escape. If this happens when I'm doing art or reading to Holly or Jack, the colours look wrong or the voices don't sound right.

Whenever I try to play dinosaurs with either Jack or Holly, I'm told in an annoyed voice,

"No Ocean you silly! The stegosaurus doesn't sound like that!"

"Sorry," I say, trying to rack my brains for the way I've done the dinosaur in question's voice in the past.

Although I try to do my work, often all I can think about is the accident.

Why did I live?

Why did Pearl have to die?

What purpose do I have on this big bustling earth, which now seems so small and quiet without most of my family?

And I still don't really want to go back to school.

There can be days on end when I don't get out of bed. Not doing stuff makes the absence of Pearl too much to handle. Sometimes I don't even want to read to Jack and Holly, which has been the main highlight of my day. I just eat, sleep and watch hour after hour of beautiful people seemingly living beautiful lives on YouTube and this only makes me want to eat and sleep more.

"I'm worried about you, you know Ocean," says Aunt Sophie one morning, when she comes into my room before work.

"I can tell that you're depressed. I'll see if I can get you a doctor's appointment. They may be able to increase the dose of your antidepressants or something?"

"I'm not depressed!" I lie. "What on earth gave you that idea?"

"I love you," says Aunt Sophie giving me a hug, which isn't quite as tight as it might be if I wasn't still recovering from my recent injury.

"Give it some thought and I'll see you later," she says, blowing me a kiss as she walks out of my room to take Holly and Jack to school and then go to work.

"Love you Ocean!" says Holly.

"Love you lots and lots and lots!" says Jack from outside my door.

"You copied me," says Holly angrily to Jack.

"No I never!" says Jack indignantly.

I'm not sure if they know why I haven't been myself for the last three weeks. I wonder what Aunt Sophie and Aunty Rose have said to them. I wonder if they'd understand. Yes, it's true, I *am* depressed. But how do you explain long term depression to a five and seven year old? Children, at that age, have emotions that change so quickly it's hard to keep up. For example: about a month ago, before I became a hermit, Jack fell over in the garden and grazed his knee. He cried as the blood dripped down his leg but he was fine once the injury had been cleaned, dressed and he had a chocolate biscuit. But injuries like mine, which come with a side effect of depression, cannot be simply made better with a hug and an Oreo.

I spend the day just listening to music and watching movies and not a huge lot else. I watch the film *Enchanted*, which was one of Pearl's favourite films. It was always her go-to movie if she was ever ill or maybe just having a bad day. She knew the entire script off by heart and the words to all the songs. None of us even laughed anymore at the funny bits because the jokes had got so old, but it's still a great film. I try to enjoy watching Amy Adams' dance around central park like someone who's escaped from a mental home, which Robert does actually say to her character at some point in the movie. But I can't feel happy. My whole life now is a dark void filled with nightmares. I've managed to put on seven kilograms in the space of three weeks! I'm shocked to see that the 'small amount of junk' I've been eating was actually quite a lot. My stomach sticks out even more than usual and my face, which was looking fairly chiseled prior to my accident with the help of orthodontic treatment, is rounder than ever. I'm disgusted by myself every time I look in the mirror. Everyday I decide that I'm going to start on a harsh, restricting diet to get as close as I can, under my circumstances, to a dream summer body. But every day by ten a.m. I realise I've eaten an entire tub of ice cream or I'm on my second packet of biscuits. Sometimes it can be both, and more. As my body gets bigger, it only makes me get more depressed and this only makes me want to eat more artery clogging rubbish.

"Can you come and play a game with me?" asks Holly every afternoon.

Every time I reply and say,

"Not right now Holly, maybe tomorrow?"

But every time tomorrow comes and I'm asked the same question I offer the same reply. I wish I *did* feel like playing with Holly and Jack, but when they ask I feel a sense of panic rising inside of my body. Panic of being seen the way I look right now by my cousins. They're only little.

They don't want to see me in this kind of state.

"Do you want to come and watch a film with us?" asks Aunty Rose every Friday evening.

"Holly and Jack really miss you."

It breaks my heart every time I refuse, because I do want to see them. But I can't. I feel like I'm becoming disconnected from my new immediate family. They, along with my happiness, seem to be becoming increasingly distant with every passing day. I wish I felt able to join in with the loud meal times or story time, but I just want to stay in my room and wallow in my grief and anxiety.

There's one evening when my depression reaches complete rock bottom. Nothing at all can bring my mood up. Not watching YouTube nor talking to Madeline and Hafsa on WhatsApp.

I've been told that my chest has now healed, which is obviously great, but I'll never be healed, not really. Even if stem-cell research becomes very advanced and they manage to grow my skin and leg back, I'll still have the emotional scars.

And I'll still have part of me missing, an external thing. My family, especially Pearl. Maybe it would be better if I ended all of it. That way I could be with them and even if there is no afterlife, at least I won't have to suffer any more.

Chapter 32

When I'm sure that everyone has gone to bed and is asleep, I quietly hop, or as quietly as I can, into the kitchen. I go over to the cutlery drawer and pull out the sharpest bread knife. I look at it and imagine making a vertical cut down the middle of my wrist. I see the thick ruby red blood pouring out my vein. I see myself lying in an ever growing pool of blood on the kitchen floor. I see myself with wide unblinking eyes.

I see... I see... I see.

But then I realise I can't do this. I know that, no matter how depressed I am, no matter what people say to me or what people do, my family would want me to grow up, finish school with good grades, be a successful artist and be surrounded by friends. I know I can't do it because of them, especially Pearl. I put the knife on the side and begin to break down. I try to keep my tears silent as they race down my face. But I can't stop the howls from escaping my mouth. I sound like a wounded dog.

It's no surprise that my cries wake both my Aunties up. They rush, blurry-eyed into the kitchen and see me in an emotional mess, on the floor, with my back against the cream coloured cupboards. I see their eyes register the knife on the kitchen side.

"Oh Ocean," says Aunt Sophie, sitting down next to me on the floor.

"Why didn't you tell me you were feeling that low? We could have organised more help for you."

"I don't know," I weep, "I suppose I didn't want to make you anxious. You've got Holly and Jack to worry about."

"You're as important to us as they are," chips in Aunty Rose sitting down on the other side of me. Their two different subtly sweet smelling perfumes mix together and is somewhat soothing.

"Thank you," I say, trying and failing to sniff my emotions back into the deep, dark cave that has become my soul, "But I feel like I'm ruining the perfect family image."

"You're not ruining anything," reassures Aunty Rose, "And nothing is perfect, it just seems perfect. It's true, in hindsight our life felt perfect, but last summer when we heard about the crash our whole life was turned upside down."

"You know," says Aunt Sophie, "I didn't sleep for almost a month. I was so worried for you when you were at your worst, and so sad that I'd lost my niece, my brother-in-law and when they told me that I'd most likely lose my sister too."

Tears are starting to roll down both of my Aunties' kind faces. It's funny seeing adults when they cry, like proper ugly tears. It's easy to forget that they have emotions that run deep, maybe even deeper, than children.

"I'm going to put the kettle on," says Aunty Rose. "I think lots of things can be made better by a nice cuppa."

My Aunties sit up with me until almost dawn. Aunty Rose produces cup of tea, after cup of tea, after cup of tea to help calm my raging emotions down. They tuck me into bed, like they tuck Holly and Jack into bed. They find Cooky, and Aunty Rose tucks my furry friend under my chin as Aunt Sophie rocks my body slowly back and forth and keeps repeating,

"There, there. It's okay, I'm here. You're okay."

Once I would have found this highly irritating, but now the repetition of the soft words in an even softer tone fills me with a glow which I've not felt since I was a very little kid. I feel safe, snug and warm. I feel more love than I've felt at any time since the accident. My two Aunties give me kiss after cuddle; they listen to my woes and reply in the perfect way. They tell me that they're both going to take a day off work tomorrow, to make sure that I'm okay. They tell me that they'll get me a doctor's appointment.

Once they've left and I'm alone, but feeling like I've got friends all around me, I hug Cooky tight. I rub my nose into his soft fur. It still has the same sweet, fluffy warm scent it's always had, and just before I fall properly asleep for the first time in ages, I realise that I've got the two best Aunties I could have ever wished for.

Chapter 33

I stare down at my thumbs. The finger nails are short and stumpy from where I've been biting them. My insomnia has returned and I have dark circles under my puffy red eyes. I glance around the CAMHS waiting room. I spot an overly cheerful octopus cushion perched on the sofa opposite. His bright and cheery features strongly juxtapose how I feel.

I don't want to be here.

There are various posters with printed titles like 'It's okay to be different?' and 'Learn to love who you are,' and 'Helpful thoughts for the day'. My brain changes the titles to fit with how *I* feel. In my head they read: 'It's never okay to be different,' and 'Learn to hate who you are' and 'Unhelpful thoughts for the day'. There's a bookshelf with various strangely irrelevant books on it. Books like: 'The History Of Fish,' and 'Flags Of The World,' and 'Learn To Name And Shame Plants.'

What kind of weirdos come here?

Sufferers of eating disorders?

Antisocial nerds with thick glasses?

Maybe adolescents who have depression after a devastating accident?

I don't want to be in a room with some patronising middle aged therapist, asking me drippy questions in an even drippier voice.

Why am I here?

I don't want to be here!

Aunt Sophie gently pats my shoulder.

"I think you're incredibly brave Ocean," she says, "You have so much to deal with."

I nod, half absentmindedly. I find myself chewing my lip like I so often do these days. I do it so much that the left side of my mouth is all swollen and sore. I constantly feel rundown and my head is too filled with darkness to even think. My increased dose of antidepressants seems to do nothing to clear my mind. Everything seems fuzzy and like I can't focus on anything.

I don't want to do this.

I am convinced that I'll hate the therapist and the session.

"Ocean Rodrigo," someone calls. I look up for a first glimpse of the person I'll be talking to for the next hour. I'm surprised to see a woman with short black hair, a nose piercing, ear-climbers and a huge purple serpent tattoo on the top part of her muscled left arm.

"Do you want me to come with you?" asks Aunt Sophie.

"No," I say, "Thank you."

I pick up my crutches and hop through the door which the woman is holding open.

"We're going into this room here," she says, pointing to a room on the right. The decor is a very calming cream.

"My name's Jade," she says, as I take a seat on a comfortable looking chair. "It's great to meet you and to start with I'm going to ask you some questions. Please be as honest as you can."

I don't want to talk.

I'm not going to talk.

"So first, how are you feeling today?"

I shrug my shoulders not wanting to give anything away.

"I understand that you probably don't want to speak to me. I understand that there's a huge stigma around coming here. But no one has to know. What's said in this room stays in this room. Okay?"

I nod.

"So how are you feeling today?"

"I've been better," I mutter.

"Why do you think that is?"

"Don't know."

"Can you describe to me how it feels to be inside your mind?"

I shake my head, not knowing if I've got the right kind of words. But then I see a biro and a piece of paper on the table.

"Can I please use these?" I ask slowly.

"Sure," exclaims Jade.

Jade watches as I draw a lonely figure floating around in a wasteland. I draw myself in a hazy landscape where everything around me is distorted and looks like it's stepped straight out of a horror movie. A table has bent legs, the walls seem too close. I even add the octopus cushion with menacing staring eyes and set of gigantic triangular teeth. I draw myself trapped in a cage, tears rolling down my face, eyes looking for something remotely cheery. But all I can see is dark clouds just waiting for the right moment to drown me in sorrowful rain. I draw my emotions as a long python wrapping itself around my neck and suffocating me before it'll sink its teeth into my scarred flesh.

I look up at Jade. She's transfixed on my sketching.

"This is good," she says, "This is very good."

"Thank you," I mutter.

"So why do you think you feel like this?"

It's kind of strange, I thought I'd not want to talk about any of this, find it too cringey and want to close up like an oyster shell. I thought that I'd want to just sit and stare into the middle distance whilst some therapist talked at me. But Jade's calming demeanor makes it easy. She doesn't force solutions on me, like take more medication or try and block these emotions out. Instead she listens and nods and gives me some coping strategies.

"Breathe in for four, hold for four, breathe out for four and hold for four," she says demonstrating as she goes.

"Of course square breathing won't solve everything, and I know that you'll still feel loss everytime you think about your family, but sometimes it helps to take a few minutes of quiet, and allow your mind to become a bit clearer."

Later that day when I'm home again I start feeling anxious and my head is filled with deep dark storms. I start to panic. Then I hear Pearl's voice.

"Come on Oceay," she says, *"Do that breathing Jade taught you. Come on, I'll help you. In for four, hold for four…"*

"Out for four," I whisper, "Hold for four."

"Good," says Pearl's voice, *"Now repeat the cycle."*

I do repeat it. I do it ten, twenty, a hundred times and eventually I find that I have far more headspace.

Chapter 34

After February half term, and after quite a few more CAMHS sessions with Jade, I finally feel ready to go back to school. I'm still building up my strength but my chest is now feeling a lot, lot better than it did. I'm still depressed, obviously, but I feel in a good enough mood to do Holly's hair in two Space Buns, as this is a hair style she hasn't learned yet.

"Wow!!!" says Aunt Sophie, "Don't you look gorgeous?"

"Yes," smiles Holly, showing off the gaps in her teeth.

"You look fantastic," agrees Aunty Rose. "And what do you say to Ocean?" she says looking up at me with a grateful expression. I know she's grateful because styling Holly's hair is a complete nightmare: she squirms, she squeals, she wriggles and she pulls.

"Thank you Ocean," says Holly, sweetly.

Hafsa, Madeline and I meet up at the school gates.

"I'm so sorry I said all that stuff," I say to the two of them. "I honestly didn't mean any of it?"

"No," says Hafsa, "We should be apologising to you."

"Yes," agrees Madeline, "We should have noticed that you weren't looking well."

"We also shouldn't have said that period pains are the worst pain ever," says Hafsa, "We can't imagine what kind of physical and emotional pain you must be going through every day."

"You don't know the half of it," I mutter.

My loyal friends don't leave my side at either break or lunchtime today.

"We don't want to risk people like Jodie taking advantage of you," explains Hafsa. Although Jodie and Amber have now been expelled it's very kind of my friends to keep me company at times which could be very lonely.

My last lesson is art and Ms Williams' smile greets me in the same cheery way it did when I returned to school in January.

"Ah Ocean," she beams, "Great to have you back."

The lesson is quite hard for me to follow as the class are part way through a topic I've never studied. It's the same with most of my subjects, but I do my best to use charcoal to draw a smoking volcano. Ms Williams comes and crouches down beside me.

"Excellent!" she exclaims.

"It's not," I shrug.

"No, it *is*," she answers back. "I see so much talent in you, Ocean. That's why I wanted to come and talk to you." She takes a deep breath.

"The Tate Modern are running an art competition. It's free to enter. They're especially interested in the work of people dealing with medical and mental health issues. I hope you don't mind, but I thought of you. If you win, your artwork will be sold at the gallery. Who knows where that might lead Ocean."

I feel my eyes widening, and almost bulging, out of their sockets at the thought.

Me... the most inconsequential person in the world... an actual selling artist?

"There's no guarantee that your work will get anywhere though," says Ms Williams, "I think this will be a highly competitive competition."

I nod. Of course, art is like a lotto draw; you could buy one hundred tickets and still most likely not win!

"It closes in two months," says Ms Williams, rising to her feet. "It's just something for you to think about."

She gives me a gentle tap on the shoulder.

"Keep going," she whispers, "This is really good."

Maybe she's right.

I look up the competition when I get home, to check it's legit. Sure enough, I find the page on the Tate Modern website. It says:

'*We are looking for artists of any age who have experienced or continue to experience complex medical and mental health issues to help us understand what the world looks like from their perspective. We are looking for expressions of hopes, fears and dreams in as wide a range of techniques as possible. For more information, click the link below.*'

"Everything okay?" asks Aunt Sophie, looking a little worried. "You've been very quiet since you got back from school. Has someone said something?"

I shake my head and turn the phone to show my Aunty the webpage.

"Oh wow!!" she exclaims. "I think you should definitely do it. I think people would come from miles to see your art. It's very insightful. I reckon in a hundred years time, people will be analysing your artwork at the highest level. They'll wonder why you used a certain technique, or why you used a certain colour..."

At that moment Holly stumbles into the room.

"Mummy?" she whines.

"Yes my angel," says Aunt Sophie, turning to face her daughter.

"I've got a bad tummy ache," she moans.

"Here." She points to her right side.

"I think you need an early night," says Aunt Sophie, leading Holly in the direction of her room. Normally my cousin would kick up a fight about being in bed by quarter to six, but today she goes with no argument. She must be feeling bad, if she goes off to bed that easily. I go into her room, five minutes later, to read her a chapter of *Candy Floss* by Jacqueline Wilson but when I poke my head round the door, she's already fast asleep with Aunt Sophie tucking her in.

"I think she's feeling the worse for wear," confirms Aunt Sophie. "I'm sure she'll be better in the morning. School's so tiring for these little ones. I'm sure it was easier in my day!"

My mind can't focus on my homework that evening. My earlier excitement about the art competition has been replaced as my mind keeps jumping to strangely sinister thoughts about Holly.

What if she's going to die? is the question that haunts my mind the most. I know it's an extreme thing to think, but I feel my entire body filling with concern over my baby cousin. Holly feels increasingly like my second baby sister with every day that passes. Jade would say this is just a trigger from my accident and bereavement but I can't shake the feeling of anxiety.

I hear Pearl's voice saying

"She'll be fine Oceay. I'll make sure of it."

Jade says it might not be the best thing to get too talkative with my dead sister, but right now it feels like the only thing that stops the overwhelming sense of dread.

"Thank you" I whisper back.

Chapter 35

When I get home from school on Friday, Holly is still ill and lying with her legs tucked up to her chest in bed.

"She's got a temperature," says Aunty Rose "And she's been sick loads today! If she doesn't improve soon, we'll have to take her to the Doctors'."

"I want my Mummies," complains Jack, who's sitting with his thumb in his mouth on the sofa in the sitting room.

"I know," I say. *I wish I could see my Mummy more too.* "But they're looking after Holly, because she's not very well."

I sit with Jack and show him some videos on my phone and download a couple of free games for him to play. I help him draw a house, surrounded by lions, dinosaurs and tigers.

"They're all friendly though," says Jack indignantly. "They want to be friends."

"Of course they do," I reply. "They want to play tennis and give you big bear hugs." This makes Jack giggle.

I am just about to go to bed when there's a loud scream from Holly's bedroom.

"My tummy really hurts!!!" she wails. I rush into her room at the same time that Aunt Sophie and Aunty Rose do. Holly is writhing around, getting herself tangled up in her green duvet.

"It hurts so, so much!" she groans. Aunty Rose takes her temperature. A worried look crosses her face.

"It's almost forty degrees," she says. For a minute she becomes more like a nurse than a mum. Her medical training kicking in, she says:

"I think this could be appendicitis, I'm going to call 999."

While Aunty Rose makes the call, I perch on the end of Holly's bed.

"Hey," I say, trying to sound calm and soothing, "I need you to be very brave. Just for a bit, until help arrives."

I stretch out my arm.

"Squeeze my hand," I say. "Yeah go on, squeeze it as hard as you like."

My cousin doesn't need to be told twice, she grips my fingers so tightly I'm worried she might cut off the circulation, but it seems to be helping her.

"Let's play a game," I suggest. "How about we take it in turns to say stuff we like? Sound good?"

Holly nods, perspiration running down her forehead.

"I'll start," I say. "Reading to you."

Holly is clearly in a lot of pain but she manages to say

"Mr Fluffy the Bear," in a small voice.

"Good," I say. "Art."

"Jack."

We play this game back and forth for the next ten minutes until help arrives. Holly repeats the items on the list a couple of times. But hey: she's ill, I know I couldn't have concentrated as well as this after my accident. She's being so brave. Aunty Rose comes and sits with her back to mine on the end of the bed, while Aunt Sophie hastily packs an overnight bag.

"Which teddy do you want?" asks Aunt Sophie, flustered.

Holly's really not well at all. She points to a giant blue fluffy rabbit, sitting next to a frog and mouse on her book case. I can see Aunt Sophie thinking about it, and wondering if the rabbit might be too big, but then she says,

"Yes. OK. Sky it is then."

The paramedics arrive and ask Holly and my two aunties lots of questions. It definitely helps that my aunty's a nurse. They nod and make notes and they agree that the symptoms are concerning. So Holly is taken into the ambulance that's waiting outside. I go into the vehicle to say goodbye and good luck to Holly. I look around and realise I don't remember either of my own ambulance rides. As a child, and probably until last year, I'd always wanted to be 'blue-lighted' somewhere! I go over to Holly and give her a big hug.

"You'll be okay." I tell her, "I'll come and see you soon in hospital. I promise."

Holly's face is as white as a sheet and her eyes are half closed, and then I'm told I have to get out of the ambulance. I get out of the back and stare with Aunt Sophie at the ambulance disappearing around the street corner.

Chapter 36

The next day is a Saturday and when I first get up Aunt Sophie is talking with Aunty Rose on the phone. She looks very worried.

"Right," she says, "OK, right, we can be there in say, an hour?"

I hear Aunty Rose's slightly muffled voice saying,

"Yeah, I need someone to talk to."

Aunt Sophie puts the phone down and sighs.

"Everything OK?" I ask, as I bite into some peanut butter on toast.

"No," says Aunt Sophie. "Holly's going in to get her appendix removed this morning. They couldn't fit her in last night for surgery, you know with the NHS being 'short staffed and overworked and underpaid.'"

I nod, recognising this quote from an episode of Casualty.

"You coming with me?" asks Aunt Sophie, heading towards her room.

"Yeah," I say. "I promised Holly that I'd come and see her today."

Aunt Sophie then says:

"I'd better call Tom's mum. She'll have to look after Jack today. I'm not sure if he'd cope seeing Holly so ill."

Just before we leave Jack runs up to me to give me a picture for Holly. It's of two people, big circles with eyes and mouths and hair and lines sticking out - possibly arms?

"I'm sure she'll love it," I say to Jack, wishing more than anything I could scoop him up and give him a big bear hug.

At the hospital we are greeted by Aunty Rose in the foyer.

"She's just gone down to theatre," she explains looking at the time. "She went under anaesthetic ten minutes or so ago."

She looks worried.

"I know this is completely mad, because I know she's in the best possible hands, but I'm worried that what's wrong with her might be quite a bit more serious than just appendicitis, which is serious enough in itself."

Aunt Sophie goes and gives her wife a hug,

"She'll be fine. They'll look after her fine. You know better than anyone how good the medics are here."

"Yeah," says Aunty Rose, trying to sniff back her concern.

"I think we should go for breakfast," I say, my stomach rumbling, despite finishing my toast just fifteen minutes ago.

"Sounds good," says Aunt Sophie "Even though I can't face anything but coffee."

We go to the hospital canteen and I get a full English with, bacon, eggs, sausage, beans, tomato and fried toast. The Whole Works. The time that we wait feels like a century. Whenever Aunty Rose's phone beeps she hastily checks the display but everytime it just says things like, 'Vodafone's new monthly deal', or 'Jack and Tom have been making cakes ever since you left' from Tom's mum. Eventually though Aunty Rose's phone rings and it is the surgical team. I see the colour draining from her face, which was looking considerably brighter after she'd had some high fat food.

"We'll be right there," says Aunty Rose, already getting to her feet and picking up her handbag.

"Her appendix had already burst by the time they got her in," she said. "Why did I not recognise the symptoms of appendicitis the other day?" Her eyes are filling with tears. "I should have known, I'm a nurse!"

"It's more difficult when it's your own family though," I offer.

"I know," says Aunty Rose as we walk, well they walk, I hop along a hospital corridor. "But if I'd left just a few more hours…"

"We can't think like that!" says Aunt Sophie.

"Yeah," I say.

How many times I've wished we'd never got in the car last summer.

We enter recovery, which is loud with beeping and general medical noise. It sounds very similar to the burns ward actually. Holly is lying drowsily on a hospital bed with a blood pressure monitor and a cannula dripping fluids into her body. She doesn't look right.

"Hey Holly," I whisper, while Aunt Sophie and Aunty Rose are speaking with the surgeon."It's Ocean here. You're being so incredibly brave, you know that? You're such a grown up, big brave girl, aren't you?"

"Ocean," says Holly sleepily.

"Shhh," I say, "Save your energy. Right now all you need to focus on is getting better. Alright hun?"

She falls back into a doze.

When she's back up on the ward I talk to her again. She's still quite drowsy and no doubt very sore but I burble on, telling her a story about Sky The Bunny going on an adventure in space. I keep changing the pronouns of the fluffy toy because I'm not sure what Holly meant them to be, seeing as Sky can be either. I tell her about how Sky meets a friendly alien called Golin and the two of them fight off the Rag invaders.

Eventually I leave with Aunty Rose, as Aunt Sophie decides to stay with Holly tonight.

"She'll be okay," I say to Aunt Sophie, patting her on the shoulder.

Chapter 37

When we arrive home Jack and Tom are playing spies in the garden. A whole load of iced fairy cakes with clumsily scattered sprinkles are on the table. Tom's mum sits on a chair, multitasking between looking at her phone and making sure Jack and Tom don't fall over in the garden.

"How is she?" she asks when we walk into the kitchen.

"She's woken up from surgery," I say.

"But..."

"But her appendix had already ruptured by the time they got her into theatre," says Aunty Rose, putting the car keys down and putting the kettle on.

"Oh my goodness," exclames Tom's mum, "How long do they think she'll be in for?" Aunty Rose shrugs her shoulders.

"Too soon to tell right now," she says, taking three mugs down from the cupboard, "I'd probably think at the end of next week or something. Now, how about we lay into some of these delicious looking cakes to take the edge off things?"

Tom and Jack must have heard the word cake and rush inside, spying games completely forgotten.

"Did you give my picture to Holly?" asks Jack excitedly, after Tom and his mum have gone home.

"Yes," I say, "Although she wasn't really well enough to look at it when I gave it to her." Jack slumps his shoulders.

"Ooh," he whines.

"But," I say, "I'm sure that when she does start to feel a little better and looks at it, she'll love it."

"OK," says Jack, and runs off to play with the dolls' house he and Holly share or something like that. I decide that I'm going to start planning my picture for the art competition. I want to paint a picture of life without Pearl, like the one I painted when I was in hospital, but a slightly different piece with the same kind of emotions.

I begin by sketching. I draw myself under water, my breath running out, my blonde wig waving in the current. The fish pass me by without a second thought. My arms are flailing all over the place as I struggle for air. I'm right at the bottom of the ocean, so there are quite a few pearls on the ocean's floor, but they're smashed up and mainly in shards. There's also algae all around my panicking body, except I draw it as looking like hundreds of disfigured hands stretching out to strangle me. My mouth is open as if I'm trying to scream but I can't.

I thought this would just be a practice sketch, not the one I send in, but inspiration seems to be pouring out. I decide to draw my finer features as they look now, as opposed to how they looked last year. I take great care when using my pastels and draw every tiny bit of skin as the burned mess it now is. Time is flying by but I don't seem to notice. I take great care in showing bits of the algae-hands as being moldy and rotting down. I also make completely sure to sketch and paint my figure as the shape it is now. I can't believe I ever complained about my appearance before the accident. I work on it late into the evening. Aunty Rose comes in at about ten and her eyes widen.

"Ocean!" she exclaims, "That is phenomenal!"

"Thank you," I say.

"No, it is though," she continues. "Is this for the competition at the Tate Modern?"

"Yes," I say, "I think so."

"It's amazing" she says, "But I think you should probably go to bed now. You had a late night last night and I was planning to go and see Sophie and Holly tomorrow, if you want to come that is?"

"Yes," I say, "Definitely." I think about my eyes and how I've been struggling to keep them open for the last half an hour. It's been worth it though. I feel as if I've created an entire visual world which expresses my feelings. The best I can do anyway.

Chapter 38

"Hi Holly!" I say, entering the ward the next morning, "How are you feeling?"

"Ocean," smiles Holly, "I feel a bit better but my belly still really hurts."

"Well it will," says Aunty Rose, sitting on the chair where Aunt Sophie was, giving Aunt Sophie a chance to go and make a cup of tea.

"You were really brave and had a big operation," continues Aunty Rose, "But it won't be long before you're home."

"I miss home," says Holly, her happy tone suddenly turned wobbly.

"And home misses you," I say. "But I've told all of your teddies that they need to give you lots of hugs when you get home again, and that won't be long."

"Really?" asks Holly.

"Yeah," I say, "But the doctors and nurses want you to be completely better before they let you go."

I think about how bored Holly must be, remembering the long days before Maris kindly gifted me her phone, when all I'd do is sometimes sketch but mainly just stare up at the ceiling and silently grieve my Dad and Pearl, worry about Mum and try to come to terms with my own injuries.

We stay for quite a few hours. Holly and I ride up and down on her bed, which I'm pretty sure every child since the invention of electrical hospital beds has done. We draw and then I start reading Holly the first book in a new series that Madeline told me her younger sister likes. I've run out of books that *I've* read to read to Holly. However, I begin to realise *The Lost Twin* might be a bit of a poor choice. The book appears to be about a girl, called Ivy, who's twin dies in 'mysterious circumstances'. Although there's nothing at all mysterious about the way that my twin died, every word feels like walking through wet sand. But I keep on reading, because Holly seems to be enjoying the book and I'm here for her not for me, so I keep going.

"Can't we keep reading," pleads Holly when it's time to go. "It's such a good story."

"We'll finish it tomorrow," I say warmly. Well, I try to sound warm, but I'm not sure how my voice actually sounds.

"See you then," I say, waving before I start hopping towards the ward exit.

When I get home I work in the living room and finish painting the scales on the distressed fish that swim past me in my picture. When I'm done I think my picture actually looks quite good.

"There's no guarantee of course that I'll hear anything back," I remind myself out loud as I pack my art supplies away.

"That's true,"' says Aunt Sophie, "But you've given yourself the best chance by entering."

I remember at my primary school, the main mantra, other than respect, inclusion and empathy was '*You have to be in it to win it.*' I remember Mr Jacobs, our Headteacher, saying this to us in an assembly once. I think he was talking about a Maths challenge, which some people in my year had entered. There's no knowing whether I'll win the Tate Modern competition but at least I'm in it!

When Aunt Sophie and I go to visit Holly in hospital the next day, she's looking a bit better and is now sitting up, although I can see she hasn't touched her lunch. To be honest, I don't blame her. The lumpy mashed potato with congealed beef mince really doesn't look very appetizing, even for someone who hasn't just had their appendix burst!

"Please can we carry on with the book Ocean?" says Holly.

As I read to my younger cousin I'm increasingly aware of the piles of homework on my desk which are due in tomorrow. I decide for now to put them to the other side of my mind. When Ivy discovers Scarlet is actually alive at the end of the first book, the story pinches at my thoughts, because there's no way that Pearl will ever come back. She's been dead for more than six months. It's been too long now for me simply to discover that she's actually in a mental institution, like in Sophie Cleverley's book.

Holly gives me a picture to give to Jack.

"It's my reply to his," she says, proudly passing me her felt tip drawing of a rabbit in a field, at least I think that's what it's meant to be.

"Well done!" I exclaim, "This is really good! I'll make sure to give it to him later on." I give Holly a gentle pat on the shoulder.

Later, when Aunt Sophie, who has once again swapped around with Aunty Rose, and I get back home I listen as Aunt Sophie and Max's mum talk about the most mundane and boring stuff ever like: mortgages and extracurricular activities for their kids. So I excuse myself and I go into my room to immerse myself in the horrors of GCSE Physics.

Chapter 39

The next week at school is about the same as any other week at school, apart from the fact that it's a four and not a five day week because of an inset day! On Tuesday, I have Art as a final lesson. We're working on our pieces themed around nature. I paint a red squirrel in a tree. It's holding a giant walnut, with a big bite taken out of it. The squirrel is choking and I draw its eyes as being wide-open and terrified.

Ms Williams walks around the classroom saying things like:

"That's really good Lilly, well done," and "Excellent work Simran, keep it up."

When she gets to me and sees the half dead rodent that I've drawn. Her eyes widen.

"Ocean… it's very good. But it's a little," she fumbles for the right word, "Sad?"

"I know," I say proudly, "But life is sad Miss."

I can see her eyes moving around, as she tries to think of an appropriate response. I try and fill in the awkward gap,

"I don't see the point in portraying life as something it's not. I'm trying to convey emotion, stuff that people can really relate to."

"Can people relate to a squirrel choking on a nut?"

"Yeah," I say, "I mean, as I say, death is everywhere. I would know." These words shock my teacher and she nods.

"Well keep going. It's certainly powerful" she encourages, as she walks over to Lola's desk to inspect her lake drawing.

My God, Lola is so boring.

I keep going with my picture, illustrating some baby squirrels nearby. Their mouths are open in helpless terror. I draw the background as being an ominous grey cloudy colour. I imagine the baby squirrels shivering with fear as an electric storm comes closer and closer to burning their treetop home down. Jade would have a lot to say about this picture in our counselling sessions!

"How was history?" I ask Hafsa as we leave for the day.

"So boring," replies Hafsa. "We're still on Crime and Punishment through time. Everyone's done with learning about night watchmen and the Hue And Cry. We all want to move onto Weimar and Germany!"

"How was Art, you two?" asks Hafsa, looking at Madeline and me.

"OK," I say rolling my eyes, "But I don't think Ms Williams liked my drawing of a choking squirrel!"

The next day is Wednesday, and I don't have any good lessons, just double Maths, Chemistry, Physics and PE (or for me, time to revise in the library). It's actually the most disgusting day of the whole week. Who even enjoys those subjects? On a Wednesday all that can keep me motivated is eating large amounts of junk food. It fuels my brain. Hafsa and Madeline complain with me at break times about their days. They both also have a day full of science lessons, but their last lessons are different.

"Oh my God!!!" moans Madeline, "I've got PSE next and we're doing the most awkward lesson." She looks at mine and Hafsa's puzzled looks.

"You know…" she says, finding it hard to let the words out, "The lesson on how to use contraception!!!"

I cringe at the words and I don't blame her. I've heard it's an awful lesson and I'm really not looking forward to it.

That evening I play noughts and crosses with Jack and let him win eighty percent of the rounds because he's so little. Anyway, the ecstatic looks on his face are definitely worth it. He squeals every time he gets three in a row and does a little victory dance all around the sitting room. I love him so much. He asks me the most strange and adorable questions like: "How old does a dinosaur live?" and "How can I get to meet Olaf the Snowman?" Everytime I try and come up with answers which will satisfy him and they always appear to make him happy.

But no matter how much I play with my younger cousin, and wish I was still five, my wish never comes true and I always have to do my homework. The velocity time graphs make absolutely zero sense to my creative brain. The problem with my mind is, it always wanders off, to the Land of Paintbrush when Dr Brown is teaching us Physics. When he explains things to me, I don't really pay attention. I just nod and say "Yeah," vaguely when he asks

"Does that all make sense Ocean?"

The thing is, Physics isn't an important subject for me to excel at. I remember Mum saying:

"Just focus on what you love," and that's what I'm trying to do, put all of my effort into painting. I'll never need to know what the chemical symbol for potassium is or how to balance a chemical equation or how to do Pythagoras (whatever that is). No, all I need to know is how to engage an art lover with my work: that's it. When will I ever need any of this academic crap? The answer is never. But I still plod on with my school work. I kind of want to prove to myself that I can get through it.

Chapter 40

On Saturday, I enter the kitchen to discover Aunty Rose on the phone to Aunt Sophie. She sounds very pleased.

"That's excellent!" she exclaims. "Wow, OK then. Well let me know when you're ready for me to come and pick you up."

She's smiling when she gets off the phone.

"Good news?" I ask, as a butter myself some toast.

"Yes," says Aunty Rose. "The doctors are happy for Holly to come home from hospital today!"

"That's great," I reply, biting into my toast which is covered in thick layers of marmite and butter.

"I know," replies Aunty Rose. "The doctors say that she'll need to be off school for a couple of weeks but they're now happy for her to recover at home."

I smile excitedly. I was so worried about Holly when she first went into hospital.

"She'll probably recover better at home. You know... now that she's been treated and all,"

"Yes," says Aunty Rose, "But one of us will always have to stay here all day. Luckily both of our work places have been very understanding. You know... with you and Holly and everything."

I think about how nice it would be to always know where your income is coming from. I remember the flaming row that Mum and Dad had the day before the crash; the anger that Mum felt towards Dad because his music business never properly took off. I wonder if Mum would have shouted at him the same way if she could have glimpsed the future.

Later, once Aunty Rose has a phone call from Aunt Sophie saying that they've been discharged she says

"You coming with us Ocean?" raising one eyebrow.

"Yeah sure," I say, heading off to find my right shoe.

On the way to the hospital Aunty Rose and I listen to Jack ramble on about school.

"Mr Bradley says we have to not push each other in the lunch hall."

"Uhm, yes well that's important isn't it Jack. Otherwise someone could get hurt," replies Aunty Rose.

"Tom was pushing one of the silly girls in our class and Mr Bradley got cross."

"Why are the girls silly?" I ask.

"All girls are silly, you silly!" says Jack.

I'll tickle him to death when we get home.

When we pull into the carpark of the hospital we see Aunt Sophie pushing Holly in one of those blue hospital wheelchairs. Holly's also got a green hospital blanket on her lap. I remember the scratchy, rough feeling of those blankets. She still doesn't look her bouncy, normal self but she looks a lot stronger than she did a week ago.

"Hey Holly, how are you doing?" I ask once she's in the car.

"Better thank you," says Holly. She's wearing a pair of black leggings and a green fleece.

'Loungey clothes,' Mum used to call them.

When we get home Holly goes immediately to her room. I squeeze into her single bed and spend the rest of the day reading and chatting and watching Disney films with her. *The Lion King* is making me cry more than it has ever done before, even as a child. I think Holly is surprised because I don't think she's ever seen me cry before. I think more than anything it's the way that Mufasa dies which makes the film so emotional for me.

Holly doesn't really feel like eating any food. Even though Aunty Rose makes her favourite homemade pizza, she's done after just one slice.

"It was really yummy," defends Holly, "It's just my tummy still hurts."

"That's OK sweetie," says Aunty Rose, hiding her hurt very well, "That just means more for us doesn't it?"

"Will you eat the rest of it?" asks Holly panicking, "I don't want the food to go to waste."

"I'll eat it," I say, thinking that the food will instead go onto my waist! After dinner I go and read a bit more to Holly. I know that I can't procrastinate over my physics revision much longer but the joy in Holly's eyes when I come into her room to read to her is worth a thousand physics GCSEs. She starts yawning very loudly after just ten minutes and asks if we can stop.

"Of course we can," I say, thinking that she must still be feeling under the weather if she's not begging me to read another chapter to her.

My brain hurts as I try to wrap my head around the equation for kinetic energy. How on earth am I supposed to remember that it's equal to 'half times mass times square velocity'? I don't even really know what those words mean. I'm completely dreading tomorrow's test. I heard Madeline saying that it helps her to make up little songs about the equations. I try and think of ways in which I could remember it. It's not like I could create a piece of art work to help me remember. I end up just having to write each equation out ten times. I'm actually not sure if it'll work but it's worth a try right?

Chapter 41

The alarm feels like it's stabbing me out of sleep when it goes off at half past six on Monday morning. I feel myself jumping out of the tranquility of sleep. I drag myself from bed and my body feels like lead. I now regret doing my homework until gone midnight. I'm not even sure if any of the information has really gone in. But the test is first thing so there's not much that· I can really do about the whole situation now. I arrive at school and enter the classroom, which the test will be in, like a warrior entering battle. I take a deep breath as I open up the assessment booklet.

"It was difficult, but ultimately I actually don't think it went too badly," I say to Madeline and Hafsa at break time.

"Well done!" says Hafsa.

"Yeah," says Madeline, "What do you think you got?"

"I'm hoping for about fifteen out of thirty, but I'll be happy to get any marks at all!"

The remaining four lessons of the day drag by. I seriously hate all subjects at school, apart from art of course. On days when I don't have art, time seems to be twice as slow as normal. The time feels like I'm trying to hop through thick mud, but my crutches keep getting completely stuck in the brown gooey stuff. Every lesson has teachers announcing things like:

"Don't forget that we have an assessment next week," and

"Don't forget your Maths homework," and

"This is one of the most important things to learn in the entire syllabus."

Whatever!

When I get home from school later that day, I'm expecting Holly to still be in bed recovering. But I'm surprised to see that she's made it to the sitting room and is lying on the sofa watching *The Dumping Ground*. This show is a total rip off of *Tracy Beaker Returns*, a show that Pearl and I watched back in the late 2000s and early 2010s. Holly's sucking her thumb, something I'm sure that she'll regret when she has to endure two years of painful braces.

"Ocean! Ocean!" she calls when I enter the room. I perch at the end of the sofa, just missing Holly's slipper-covered feet.

"How are you feeling?" I ask.

"Loads better now. I've just watched movies today," she explains.

"Lucky you!" I reply, with mock surprise. "When you're at secondary school like me, if you're ill you can't just watch films. So enjoy your time at primary for as long as it lasts. You'll really miss it."

I'm not really sure if Holly listened to my words of wisdom because she's immediately onto the next topic of conversation.

"Anyway," she burbles, "When I'm better Olivia is going to come round to play."

"OOO!" I say, "That sounds fun!"

"Yeah," says Holly excitedly, "We're going to make biscuits!"

Holly's innocence is adorable. It's difficult to describe how much I love her.

I am able to finish my homework before dinner as I only have two pieces to do, English and History. This enables me to watch telly with Holly. I introduce Holly to the film *Inside Out*, which I can't believe she'd never seen before. Her high pitched laugh at the funniest bits creates a warm glowing feeling inside. Her laugh is the kind of laugh that makes you want to laugh along with her. It's more infectious than the flu.

"Oh my God," I say the next day at break time to Hafsa and Madeline, "My cousin is so, so cute."

"My younger cousin is so irritating," moans Hafsa looking at her phone. "I thought it's the law that younger cousins, or siblings for that matter, are meant to really get on your nerves."

"Yes, well Holly and her brother can be annoying too, but on the whole they're super adorable," I explain.

"Look," I say, "I've got a picture of me with the two of them. Don't you think they're like so gorgeous."

"Yeah, I guess that they're quite sweet," says Madeline, uninterested.

The rest of the week is actually not that bad. There's just a few assessments, which are obviously a bit gross, but art lessons are amazing because we are working on painting a picture of people we love. I paint my whole family: Mum, Dad, Pearl, Holly, Jack, Aunty Rose and Aunt Sophie.

"I see no reason why I can't paint people who aren't here any more," I explain to Ms Williams, when she looks surprised at my picture.

"It's very good," she says, "But I wonder if it looks a bit cramped, with all these people in it. Maybe in future only paint one person?"

"OK," I say nodding, although I have no intention of alteringing my style.

"She told me basically to change it!" I rant in the playground. "You know, I don't think *she* can talk, her art work has got no style."

"I think she's OK really," says Madeline slowly. "But yes, I can understand why that would be irritating for you, given that you're very talented at art."

"Sometimes…" I say, holding back my rage, because I'm trying to not ruin my friends' break time,

"…Teachers really annoy you?" suggests Hafsa, her brown almond shaped eyes gleaming.

"Yeah," I say, "They're so irritating!"

On Friday afternoon for some reason I feel extremely tired, like I did when I first returned to school in January. I collapse on the sofa with Holly for an hour and decide that homework can wait. My excuse for not starting work yet, to myself, is that I'm spending time with my cousin who's been ill.

"Are you still alright to come and visit your mum tomorrow?" asks Aunt Sophie.

Mum's now been settled in a long term care facility. With all the work at school and worrying about Holly I've been keeping this at the back of my mind. There's only so much I can stress about to be honest.

I have an early night, getting into bed at nine, but it takes me ages to get to sleep because of the anxiety building up inside me about visiting Mum.

What will it be like?

Does she like it there?

Is there any way at all to tell?

These questions come with me on my journey into sleep.

Chapter 42

When Aunt Sophie and I drive into Clear Water Residential Home, I'm surprised to see that there's a whole lot of greenery.

"I was expecting it to be... OK," I whisper to Aunt Sophie, "But this is stunning!"

"Yes," says Aunt Sophie as she turns off the engine, "That's why I chose this particular one. Your garden was very green. Whenever your Mum had a day off from work she'd spend the whole day in the garden. Do you remember?"

I do remember.

I remember all the sweet scented flowers and the fresh and cool smell of the newly cut grass. I remember the busy bees loved our garden, and would spend all summer collecting pollen from the roses, nasturtiums and tulips.

The air around the residential home smells clear and healthy, good for someone like Mum with 'potential respiratory issues' like the doctor said. There's a flat path leading up to the automatic-door at the entrance. The tarmac is surrounded by grass and every few metres there's another tree. I can hear a fountain to my right. When I catch sight of it I'm awed by the utopian image. The water is clear and beautiful.

I smile as Aunt Sophie and I go in.

"Hi," says Aunt Sophie to a passing nurse, "I'm here to see my sister again and this is her daughter..."

"Ocean," I finish, looking around at the calming baby-blue and white walls.

"Come with me," says the nurse, gesturing for us to follow him.

As I hop through the corridors I become aware that people aren't looking at me. When I go to hospital, I'm used to absorbing the stares. Children point and whisper:

"Mummy what happened to that girl's leg?" A reply is rarely given until I've gone round the corner.

"Your Mum's in here," says the nurse, showing us into a white room with a hospital-like bed in the middle.

"Your Mum's supporting her own breathing very well today," a middle aged female nurse informs me. "Come, sit down," she continues, pointing to two chairs, one on either side of Mum's bed. I take the blue chair with a long back on Mum's left.

"Hello Mum," I say softly once both nurses have left, "It's me, it's Ocean."

I'm not sure if she's actually heard me in between her endless chain of dreams. Regardless though I carry on talking.

"Mum, it's me." My voice begins to crackle with emotion.

"Hi there Milly," says Aunt Sophie, "It's me, it's Sophie, your sister. It's me," I can tell that she's desperate for some kind of response but one never comes.

We sit and talk at Mum for quite a while. We tell her all about everything, apart from my psychological blips of course. We tell her about school and work, Holly and Jack, my painting and how I enjoy reading to my cousins. I describe my picture which I've bought with me, the one for the competition that I'm planning on posting later today. But neither me nor Aunt Sophie can know for sure if Mum can hear our words. We struggle to stay strong and keep the storm of tears from pelting down our faces. We both give Mum gentle hugs when we're about to leave.

"I'll be back soon to see you okay?" soothes Aunty Sophie, in the way she does when she is being one hundred percent positive.

"Love you Mum," I say waving as I exit the door, before realising that the small hand movement is completely worthless, seeing as she's permanently asleep and locked inside a world of never ending dreams. I wonder if she can remember the crash. I wonder if she also wants to wake screaming from the nightmares but can't. I hope for her sake that she's just having endless dreams about warm summer sand and Mr Whippy ice creams.

But I'll never know.

Aunt Sophie and I have to take a moment to compose ourselves once we've got back into her car. Aunt Sophie wipes the tears from her green eyes with a tissue.

"When we were little she was the cool, confident older sister. But now she's... well she's..."

We both stare into the middle distance, seeing only the grassy grounds, for a minute.

"Well," says Aunt Sophie, "We'd best be heading."

"Right, yes," I say, my mascara, which I haven't worn recently running down my face.

"I put it on for Mum," I explain to Aunt Sophie, "But there was no point really was there?"

"Well, I think that you're looking beautiful," reassures Aunt Sophie. "And if it makes you happy it's definitely worth the effort."

Aunt Sophie always manages to say the exact right thing. She knows how to respond to anything that you may tell her and her response is always said softly and in a calm and kind manner.

Chapter 43

The residential home is only a ten minute drive away from my Aunties' house so it doesn't take us that long to get back. When we get inside Holly and Jack are squabbling over the red crayon.

"It's mine," says Jack angrily.

"Yeah?" retorts Holly, "But I had it first."

They snatch back and forth.

"I'll tell you what we'll do," says Aunty Rose, "Jack you can use it first and then Holly you can use it. How does that sound?"

I leave the kitchen with a smile on my face. I go into my room and take out my painting, which I've wrapped in a protective plastic cover to prevent any damage. I take out some lined paper and start to write my letter to accompany the art work.

"Dear Sir / Madam," I begin, "My name is Ocean Rodrigo and ever since I can remember I've always wanted to be an artist." I then proceed to explain about my situation and what's happened to me since last summer. I wonder if this competition is like the X-Factor and people get in if they have a good sob story but no talent. I doubt it will be like that though. Hopefully they will be more interested with the content as opposed to the story behind it. I close the large envelope Aunt Sophie found for me and write the address on it. I then add a 'Do not bend' note on the back. If they like my work, this could make my dream come true and I could at last be a selling visual artist.

"Could you please post this while you're in town tomorrow?" I ask Aunt Sophie, passing her the envelope.

"Yes, of course," she says slowly, taking it from me.

Good luck I think to myself, sending all good vibes to it.

Holly then appears.

"Ocean, can you watch a film with me?"

"I'd love to Holly, but I've got a big maths test coming up and I should really be doing...."

I look up. Holly is doing one of those teddybear style pouts, sticking out her bottom lip. I'm just about managing to resist. But then she says,

"Oh please Ocean!" Her doey eyes are too much.

"Oh okay then. I can do that later once you're in bed."

"Yay!" says Holly, jumping in the air. "Ow," she says, forgetting for one second about the three deep scars on her stomach.

"So what do you want to watch?" I ask her looking through the DVD cupboard. "There's *Shrek* or *Lassie Come Home* or..."

"I want to watch *FROZEN!*" says Holly defiantly.

"Ok, it's your choice," I mutter. I remember back in late 2013 all the way to mid 2015 all that anyone would talk about was *Frozen*. The school talent show would be almost completely made up of groups of children singing '*Let It Go*', or '*Do You Want To Build a Snowman?*'. I've completely boycotted the film for the last few years. I watched it enough times for the story line to get old.

Holly seems to really enjoy watching a snowman singing about summer and loves the fact that it's snowing in July. But all that I keep on thinking is: isn't his whole thing basically about climate breakdown? Climate change wasn't particularly on most people's radar when *Frozen* first came out but I do my best to hide my worries and enjoy the movie with Holly.

After the end of the film, where the weather returns to exactly how it was and everyone is happy, I have to go and start studying for my maths test on Wednesday.

Why is maths is so hard?

I leave Holly playing on Aunty Rose's iPad and go into my room. I stare in horror at the list of things that I need to revise. The majority of this stuff I've never even been taught because it was covered when I was not in school. Questions about the maths topics surge around my mind.

"What is standard form?" and

"How do I write things to a number of significant figures?"

The maths feels like a maze with no clear exit, or any exit at all. My brain goes round in circles for three hours. Just when I think I'm about to get out of the mathematical labyrinth, I'm faced by yet another dead end. At some point I throw down my maths book and go and find someone to complain to.

"I hate Maths!" I yell at a bemused Aunt Sophie, who doesn't deserve to be talked to like this.

"I won't ever need to know about 'Soh Cah Toa' or whatever the hell it's called!"

"I understand," says Aunt Sophie in a soothing voice, "I felt the exact same way when I was at school. But remember all that you need is a pass."

"Yes I know," I say through gritted teeth, "It's just that both my friends are predicted, like, nines."

"It's hard when you've got friends like that," my Aunt replies, "But you can't work any harder than you are working so we'll be proud of you whatever you get. Now you've had a long day, why don't I make you some hot chocolate and then you can go to bed. How does that sound eh?"

I nod.

"Sounds lovely" I say.

The hot chocolate feels like liquid gold as it runs down my throat - hot, rich and creamy. It's not long after that I'm in bed looking up at the white ceiling, wondering if Mum ever wakes up enough to do the same. Finally I hear Pearl's voice.

You'll be fine Oceay, I promise.

Chapter 44

Maths is like a vicious tarantula. It sneaks up behind you and attacks you before you notice. It bites you hard, spearing its toxic venom into the blood of its mortal prey. The half dead victim's final thoughts are of compound interest and circle theorem. They try to scream but all that comes out is ramblings of quadratic equations, which the people around don't realise is a desperate cry for help.

I take great pleasure in drawing this scene. The spider is covered in mathematical symbols and the victim has πr^2 written on their forehead. I decide that all mathematical symbols were once functioning human beings, but then they got bitten by the Mathematical Spider and they died and turned into a series of weird symbols and numbers, spending the rest of eternity haunting maths students all over the world.

"I like maths," says Holly in a perfectly innocent, but hugely infuriating way, as she does her maths homework which is colouring in all the odd numbers on a grid. "I don't know why you don't Ocean."

"It's hard," I say, "But you want to be a doctor right?"

"Yeah."

"So you need to try your best at maths okay?"

"Okay," replies Holly, slightly confused.

"Maths gets more difficult Holly," I explain, "When you're at secondary…."

"You mean big school?"

"Yes all right, big school," I say, corrected, "And for most university courses you need to pass maths. So work hard at Maths,"

"OK," says Holly. "I'm going to go and play on the swing in the garden. Can you come and play with me?"

"I'm so sorry Holly but as I said I've got a mountain of revision to do." Holly looks a bit upset. But I am astonished to hear her say the words,

"OK, work hard." She then giggles and walks off. There's no way I would have been so understanding when I was seven years old.

I continue to revise and attempt to understand the concepts. But the numbers simply fly in front of my face like tiny viruses, ready to infect the unfortunate maths student. Whether they pull through or become a mathematically obsessed zombie can only be known with time. But the symptoms of the GCSE Maths Virus are very serious. If you are badly infected your entire thinking system is dedicated to thoughts about really advanced number theory, which I really don't care about.

"I'm legit gonna fail this test," I tell Hafsa and Madeline on Wednesday, just before the torture of the Maths test begins.

"You did alright on the Physics."

"Yeah I know but I kind of understood some of that physics. With this Maths I don't have a clue!"

"Does it really matter what you get in this test? It's just an assessment and they don't really matter do they?" says Madeline taking a sip from her chocolate milkshake. "The real GCSEs are a year away. Roll on 2020!"

"I suppose so," I say quietly, "But it'll still be super embarrassing if I don't get any marks at all, which is what is going to happen."

"Like we keep saying," says Hafsa, "As long as you get a five at the end of year eleven you'll be fine. You want to do a Fine Art course anyway right?"

"Yeah," I nod, thinking about the sacred day when I'll never have to do any more boring Maths or Science again. Once I've got my GCSE in Maths, blue sky will appear and the birds will sing their beautiful sweet song. A song about better days to come, days where all I have to do is my art work and nothing else. I try to imagine a timetable where there's no Chemistry or English on it, but I can't picture it. There's something blocking my view of it, like a blackout blind or something.

The bell goes and I'm forced to leave the safety of the bench and separate from my best friends.

"Good luck," says Madeline, giving me a gentle pat on the back.

"Yeah," adds Hafsa, "You'll be fine."

"And even if you don't, no one will think badly of you," says Hafsa waving, as her and Madeline walk off to the higher tier test where they'll most likely get one hundred percent or thereabouts!

I enter my Maths classroom and I see the papers on the table. They're little grenades, waiting to blow up the students in the class.

"Right," says Mr Plat, "You have fifty minutes to complete this Maths test. You may begin."

I open the question booklet, which sits on the table in front of me. I sign my name in the box and write my teacher and class name. I then look at the first question in the booklet.

It says:

'Write 0.0089 in standard form."

My mind is blank.

Any knowledge I may have had two minutes ago is wiped away, like I've had my memory cleared of everything. The harder I try to think about how to work out standard form, the harder it is to think about anything at all.

The minutes are ticking by. I hear the other people in the class turning the pages of their Maths test but still I stare at question one, part one of a seventeen question assessment. The tap-taps of the pens around me just put me off even more. They put me off because I know that I'll do the worse out of everyone in my bottom set class. I wonder how Pearl would do in this test? We'd probably have tried to help each other revise. She was so much more academic than me.

The time is getting closer and closer to when I should be finishing the test but still my answer booklet is completely empty. I hastily write down a number which I think may answer at least one of the marks in the two mark answer.

"Right year 10," says Mr Plat, raising his scary dark eyebrows, "Put your pens down and close the paper."

All around me there are great sighs of relief.

I hear

"Thank God for that!"

And

"I'm glad that that's over!"

I, however, am anything but pleased. I mean sure, the test is over now but I've got a maximum of two percent in the entire paper. How will I ever pass this GCSE? It's a nightmare.

As Mr Plat goes around the classroom I feel anxiety starting to rise in my chest. It feels like I've got an elastic band around it, which gets tighter and tighter the closer to my desk my Maths teacher gets. He'll shout at me, scream at me for sure because he'll say "You didn't even try Ocean." But that's not true. I slaved every evening to revise like mad, giving up time I could have spent with my cousins or doing something to take my mind off my depression. His footsteps, inching nearer and nearer, my fate seconds away. He's now just one desk away, talking to Daisy.

"I tried," gabbles Daisy, "But I just didn't know the answers to any of the questions or how to work them out!"

She is fixed by a stony glare from Mr Plat. Daisy shuts up. Mr Plat approaches my desk. He flips through the test to discover that only one part of one question has been answered.

"Did you find this test difficult, Ocean?" he asks, in the patronising tone almost everyone uses towards me now that I'm missing one leg.

"Yes," I say, nodding sheepishly. I hold my breath, waiting for the stern look, bracing myself for the shouting, preparing myself for the permanent expulsion. But instead Mr Plat just nods.

"That's alright. Don't worry. I'm holding catch up sessions three lunchtimes a week starting after Easter,. If you wish to come, let me know."

"That'll be great," I say, smiling with relief.

"I'll let you know what days once I've found out what days the others are free. Have a nice Easter break," he says, walking off.

"I've legit just failed that test!" I rant at Hafsa and Madeline later.

"You don't know that," says Hafsa, trying to comfort me.

"Yes I do," I snap, "I only answered one part of a two mark question, so yeah, I'm pretty sure that's a U!"

"I think it's ridiculous that people like you, who have no interest in Maths, should be forced to endure two whole years of mathematical torture," says Madeline angrily.

"Look," says Hafsa, "I'm sure that not many other people who've had a year like you would be doing as well as you."

"Thanks." Pearl would say the same thing.

That evening I feel like a pinata that's had all the sweets and plastic crappy toys knocked out of it and is just left flat on the ground, covered in punctures all the way around it's deflated body. I lie on the sofa all evening. My excuse is that,

Number one: I've just completed a God-awful Maths test and,

Number two: I have no more homeworks to hand in before the end of term so there's nil point.

When Holly asks me to come and draw a picture with her I nod and say,

"I'll be there in five minutes."

We draw for nearly an hour solid. Holly giggles at my drawing of a big bear roaring at a little bear.

"She's being friendly to her cub," I explain to Holly. "She's actually asking her cub what he wants for dinner!"

"What *does* he want for dinner?" asks Holly, genuinely interested in a comment I made up on the spot.

"Honey sandwiches or berry biscuits," I say eventually.

"I like berry biscuits best," says Holly happily.

"Yeah," I agree, "They are pretty good aren't they?"

The last two days of term go by just like any other two days of school, except the difference is that after them there's a two week long holiday. Finally the last bell rings.

"You got any plans?" asks Madeline, as we dawdle to the gate.

"No not really," says Hafsa, "Because Ramadan will be starting at some point in the Easter holidays and I doubt I'll want to do all that much."

"Fairs," says Madeline, "What about you, Ocean?"

I shrug.

"Probs not much either. Hey if you're not doing anything we should meet up!"

"Yeah," says Hafsa, "Maybe on Monday?"

"That sounds great!" says Madeline.

"I can't wait," I say.

"Come to my house," says Hafsa. "I've got this new craft kit Ocean, you'll probably be really good at it."

"Cool," I say.

"See you Monday then?" says Madeline.

"See you Monday," smiles Hafsa. They walk off down the street as I get into Aunty Rose's car, totally ready for the Easter break.

Chapter 45

I spend that afternoon in the garden with Holly and Jack. I sit on one of the white painted benches and watch the two of them playing tag. It's like they've got a never ending energy supply, although admittedly it's most likely fueled by the amount of chocolate they've eaten since they got home. They are seriously acting like they are under the influence of drugs!

I sketch as I watch them playing. I decided to draw something with a more innocent and childish form to some of my other art. I sketch a rabbit sitting with a baby chick, still sitting in half a cracked egg shell, and a lamb, half asleep, holding a baby bottle to its lips and gently sucking. The group of animals are lying on a hay bale. Later I use my pastels and paints to give the lamb wide, pleading, blue eyes. The chick is bright yellow, with excited, black, beady eyes and the rabbit is a caramel brown, with one of its ears sticking up and the other down.

Back in my darker mood I realise the chick and lamb are completely unaware that it's only a matter of time before they're served up on a plate with roast potatoes and vegetables. But I don't mention that as I show the picture to Holly and Jack who have finally slowed down and are sitting on the grass.

"Three days until the Easter Bunny comes!" says Jack excitedly.

"I know," I say, with mock surprise. "What are you going to ask for?"

"I want a chocolate egg," says Jack.

"They're all chocolate you silly," interrupts Holly.

On Easter Saturday I don't get out of bed until eleven. I find I can think best before I've got out of bed. I think all about this time last year. Pearl and I came over to see Aunty Rose, Aunt Sophie, Jack and Holly and created an Easter egg hunt in the garden for them. We gave them both little plastic medals, which I know for a fact they both still have in prize position in their rooms. It was Pearl's idea, she was that kind of person. On Easter Day last year, we went to church. Our family aren't in any way particularly religious but at Christmas and Easter we always went. Both Pearl and I always found it extremely boring. Mum and Dad would tell us that when we were 'a bit older' we'd like it more, but that 'like', for sitting through long sermons and singing along to hymns, which you think are about to finish but then the organ starts up again, never came.

I snap back into the present when Holly and Jack skip into my room.

"Ocean? Ocean?" yells Holly, shaking me. "Are you sick, because if you are mum says that you should stay in bed? But if you're not ill I say that you should get up and stop being a lazy bones!"

"Okay! Okay!" I say rubbing my eyes. "I'm not ill, so I'm coming."

"That was very naughty of you two," lectures Aunt Sophie. "You should have left Ocean to have a lie in."

She then sighs and says under her breath,

"I'm sure you'll both want lie-ins at the weekends and holidays when you're her age."

She gives me a plate with a pancake on it. It's covered in sugar and lemon, just the way that I like it.

"It should be the best one," explains Aunt Sophie, "I've never made this batter before and I used the kids and Rose as my guinea-pigs this morning. I hope it tastes alright."

I take a giant bite of the fried batter. The texture is perfectly soft and the sugar and lemon enhance the subtle flavour perfectly.

"It's amazing!" I confirm.

"I can see you liked that," says Aunt Sophie, "You've wolfed it down!"

Aunt Sophie and I go and visit Mum. She lies there in the same listless way that she always does, eyes closed and silent. She doesn't know the date; she wouldn't know whether it was August or April. She's simply frozen in a white empty world. In the real world she might still be doing the job she loved. We could still be living in our family home. Pearl could still be alive and being the kind, wonderful and beautiful person that she was. Perhaps Mum is thinking about an imaginary world which she's queen of. Or, most likely, she's not thinking about anything specific because she's in that white cloudy place where I was before I woke up. Except that she won't ever fully wake up.

"Happy Easter," I whisper in her ear just before I leave with Aunt Sophie. Like before, I have no way of knowing if the words are even computing in her brain.

"I love you forever Milly," says Aunt Sophie.

Chapter 46

"Happy Easter!" squeals Holly, throwing herself onto my bed the next morning, jumping me from my peaceful slumbers.

"Happy Easter," I yawn, turning over onto my other side to try and escape Holly's rambling chatter.

I'm not ready for this yet.

"The Easter Bunny got me a chocolate egg!" says Holly. "Ocean? Are you awake?"

"No," I say, "I want to sleep for another hour or so."

"But it's so late. It's like half past eight." I hear her picking up a pillow, she's probably about to hit me on the head with it. I'm not sure if she understands that I don't want to enjoy Easter because Pearl can't enjoy it with me.

"You've got an Easter egg too," says Holly. "The Easter Bunny has got you an egg too! Isn't he nice Ocean?"

"Yay," I say slowly, still half asleep. "Creepy concept though," I mutter.

"What?"

"Nothing."

"Come and play with me!" she demands. "Please…" she adds.

I emerge from the safety of my duvet about fifteen minutes later and eat some of my Easter egg which I found on my bedside table. The milk chocolate melts in my mouth like a complete dream come true. A river of pure gold. It tastes fabulous. When I'm ready to get out of my bed, I realise that I've already consumed half of it.

"Oops," I say, staring at the half empty packet. "Fat life here we come."

I feel like days such as Easter and Christmas are simply write offs for dieting and healthy eating. I think about my sister. She should be here, getting fat with me. She should have chocolate all the way around her mouth, the way that she always did when she'd eaten chocolate of any sort. There's a picture, somewhere, of her on our second birthday. Her chops, and their surroundings, are covered in chocolate and she never really grew up in that department. It pains me to think about her love for chocolate muffins and how we would have made some yesterday if she were still here and she would have eaten loads already. But she's not here. I wanted to stay asleep because I was dreaming that she was still alive and well. But her voice, her appearance, an exact mirror image of how I used to be, is fading away from my mind a little bit more every day.

I go into the kitchen and I can see through the double door that Aunty Rose and Aunt Sophie are sitting on reclining chairs in the garden. I decide to go back to my room and have a shower before I go out to join them.

"Hi there, Ocean," says Aunty Rose.

"Hi," I say, "I thought you had a shift up at the hospital today?"

"I do," says Aunty Rose, "But I'm on night shifts right now."

I nod.

"It's been a couple of years since you haven't had a day shift on Easter Sunday hasn't it?" I say pouring myself some pineapple juice from the outside table in front of me.

"It's true," says Aunty Rose, taking a sip of her black coffee. "Did Holly come and wake you up this morning?" she asks.

"Yeah," I say.

"I'm so sorry," says Aunty Rose, "You know that they get excited about things like this."

"Yeah," I reply, sipping the sweet tasting juice. "But it's OK, honest. I probably needed to get up at some point soon!"

The rest of the day goes by with the soft, late spring breeze blowing through the trees in the garden. We eat Easter lunch, which is delicious. We play board games and we make chocolate rice crispy cakes like Pearl used to love. I feel as though I need to make up for the portions of the cake that she won't be eating so I stuff myself. I must eat about ten in total over the course of the afternoon.

That evening as I lie in bed, I think about the day I've had.

"It was amazing Pearl," I whisper into the empty unknown of the darkness. "You would have loved it so much." Just as I'm falling asleep I hear her voice saying,

"One day we'll have Easter together again. One day... one day..."

Chapter 47

The Easter holiday is over far too soon and before I even know it I'm back in the prison which is GCSE curriculum. It's back to five dragging lessons in a painfully slow day. Unsurprisingly I completely fail my maths test, getting just one out of fifty. Although I'm not expecting any better, the score 'one out of fifty' feels like a hard punch. It's kind of stupid but I guess that I was hoping that some kind of exam magic might have transformed my terrible effort into a better grade. But every time that I hope for magic to occur I'm reminded that magic is just a fairy tale, a cruel lie told to children when they can still believe in it.

Even Art lessons seem to be in complete slow motion. Every second on the clock feels like ten. I don't like the topic which we've started this term. I don't enjoy painting bowls of fruit for hours and hours on end. Every lesson I expect Ms Williams to announce that we've finished the still life project but that amazing day doesn't come until the end of May.

The only thing that keeps me going through these long drawn out days is talking to Madeline and Hafsa at break times. We always seem to have something to laugh about, whether it's something a teacher said in the last class or a stupid video we watch on YouTube. At the end of every break time we pretend to cry, using our '#amazing-drama-skills'. Not!

"Please," I say, pretending to cry, "You can't leave me!"

"I'm sorry," says Madeline, in the same overly emotional way, "But they're taking me away to the hell that is 'A Thousand Years of Crime and Punishment.'"

"We may never see each other again," adds Hafsa, "Because we might die of complete boredom in the next lesson."

Every time though we miraculously make it through and meet up again at break.

One afternoon in early June Madeline announces,

"So you guys know how it's my birthday in two weeks?"

"Yeah," say both myself and Hafsa. Madeline's birthday parties ever since year seven have been the event of the year, progressively getting better and better and probably progressively more expensive for her parents.

"Well," continues Madeline, "Can you guys come bowling on the day after my birthday?"

"Sure," I say, checking my digital calendar to make sure there's nothing else on which will clash with it. I'm secretly quite surprised with how low key Madeline is going this year for her birthday. Last year her parents hired out a hall and a DJ and most of our year was there. It was an amazing evening. Pearl was there too.

"Yeah I can come too," confirms Hafsa. "What time on the fifteenth were you thinking?"

"Does twelve work?" offers Madeline, raising one of her pencilled in eyebrows.

"Cool," I say, adding the event into my phone.

* * *

"I don't know what I should get for her," I explain to Aunt Sophie later that evening, "She always gets me really amazing stuff. And she's been such a great friend to me of late so I want to get her something incredible."

"I see your point," says Aunt Sophie, nodding. "I mean, she's such a kind person, both her and Hafsa are. I think she deserves a good gift for her birthday. You've got a while to think about it and find something nice haven't you?"

"I s'pose," I say, trying to rack my brains for something special to give to Madeline.

Holly comes in at that moment in her bunny rabbit pyjamas and with her hair in a plaited bun, the way that I taught her to do it.

"Look Ocean, I did it all by myself."

"Well done," I smile, turning my full attention to Holly's impressive first attempt at a fairly difficult hair style.

"Did you find it tricky?" I ask her, looking at the intricate ridges.

"No," says Holly, shaking her head so defiantly that the hair starts to come out of place.

"Wow! I found it so hard the first time that I did it," I confess. "It's amazing for a first attempt but keep practicing and it'll be even better. Cause you know what they say... practice makes..."

"Perfect," finishes Holly proudly.

"That's right," I say getting up from the sofa. "Are you ready for me to read to you now?" I'm already heading in the direction of her room.

"Yeah," says Holly, running quickly in front of me.

I start reading Holly *Emily Windsnap*. It's about a human girl who one day discovers, in her first ever swimming lesson, that she's half mermaid and grows a tail as soon as she's submerged in water. I can't believe that she'd gotten to the age she had and not discovered that she's basically half fish! It's actually an okay book though, it turns out over the next week. Emily's Mum (a human) and Dad (a merman) had a summer romance. The Dad then left the Mum pregnant with a cross species of sorts.

In this week I also finally work out what I should get Madeline for her birthday.

"She's creative like me and she likes products," I explain to Aunty Rose and Aunt Sophie, who've been pondering with me, "So I think I should get her a make your own products sort of kit. What do you think?" They both nod their approval.

"Sounds amazing," says Aunty Rose, "I'm sure she'll love it."

"Yeah," I say, "I'm gonna order it from Hobbycraft later today."

I find a bath bomb making kit for twelve quid.

"It's a lot of money for a craft kit," I think as I click on the 'add to your basket' link,

"But she's worth every penny."

Chapter 48

The Friday of Madeline's birthday is an inset-day so I type into our WhatsApp chat: *Happy birthday Mads, C U tomorrow with your present.*

Hafsa includes a selfie: *Happy birthday - Me too*

I'm secretly worried that the kit won't arrive in time but there's still tomorrow's post.

Me: *So what have you got so far for your B day?*

There's a pause and I can see Madeline is typing:

Make up, new paint brushes, nail varnish and vouchers

I text back: *Nice*

Hafsa: *Awesome*

Madeline finishes: *C u guys tomorrow at 12 x*

* * *

"It arrived," says Aunt Sophie later that evening, looking at a text message, "Paddy next door took it in. I'll go and get it."

"Thank goodness" I say, relief flooding over me. I was beginning to worry I would be turning up empty handed. When I open it up, after Aunt Sophie returns from the neighbours, I see the craft kit is absolutely perfect for Madeline. It contains: all the key fizzing bath bomb ingredients, an array of different special dyes and a selection of scented oils.

On Saturday I meet with Hafsa and Madeline in lane six of the local bowling alley. It's cool because it has a chair you can sit in as you bowl if someone has any kind of physical disability.

"Strike," I scream, throwing my arms in the air in celebration. I see my score overtaking Hafsa and Madeline's.

Pearl was far better at bowling than me. Whenever we'd go bowling she'd always win by a mile, overtaking me right from the start of the game. She'd do a little dance shaking her hips and singing

"Yeah I won, I won. Yeah, yeah, yeah!"

In the end Hafsa ends up winning both rounds. I guess it's all the cricket she plays. I thought that Madeline would be bitter about not winning at her own birthday party but she doesn't seem to care. I know that it would irritate me!

"Pizza Time!" announces Madeline, pointing to the cafe behind us. All that exercise has made me feel very hungry.

"The veggie burger please," I say pointing at the item on the menu.

"Sure," says the waiter writing it down on his notepad, "And would you like fries with that?"

Once we've all ordered, Madeline gets down to business.

"Right," she says excitedly, "I'm going to open these gifts now."

She opens Hafsa's gift first. It's a picture of her art work pasted onto a canvas bag.

"Do you like it?" asks Hafsa, worried.

"Are you kidding me?" exclaims Madeline, "I love it so much. Thank you!" She gives Hafsa a big hug.

"Now I realise why you wanted all those pictures of the paintings I've been doing in art."

"Now your gift," says Madeline to me, slowly opening the wrapping paper. "I kind of don't want to rip it," she explains, "Because if it's not ripped I can reuse the paper right?"

"Good idea," I say thoughtfully. I've got that 'will she like my present?' feeling.

"Oh my God!" smiles Madeline once she's opened it. "I've always wanted one of these. Thank you so much!"

"You're very welcome," I say, relieved that my gift choice has been a success.

* * *

"Did you get a party bag?" asks Holly later that afternoon, jumping up and down.

"No," I admit. "Party bags aren't so much of a thing after a certain age."

"That's so stupid," says Holly angrily. I know that secretly she was hoping for some sweets from my nonexistent goody bag.

Madeline sends us a picture later that night on our group chat. It's of her holding the bag that Hafsa got her. The bag appears to be filled with something.

The caption of the photo says:

Storing my homemade bath bombs in my beautiful new shopping bag. These are such amazingly thoughtful gifts. Thx so much for today xxx

I reply with a smiley emoji with heart shaped eyes.

Later that evening I lie in bed and think, like I do most nights. I think about what the day would have been like if Pearl was still here. Would there have been a third more fun and laughter than there was today? Would Hafsa have still won the bowling? Or would Pearl have beaten all of us by a mile like she did at our fourteenth birthday party? I ponder this as I go to sleep. I go round and round in mental circles until, just as I'm drifting off, I reach the same conclusion that I always do which is:

I have no way of knowing because Pearl still isn't here. She's dead and she's been dead for almost a year now.

Chapter 49

The next week at school is just as boring as the last one. I'm given what feels like a never ending chain of tests. I sit an assessment on Monday, Wednesday and Thursday. It never seems to stop.

"If this is bad," I say, "What will the end of year ten mocks be like in a few weeks?" Hafsa and Madeline shrug,

"It'll be a shit show," admits Madeline.

"Not having missed any school this year, I'm finding these tests difficult," adds Hafsa, "So goodness knows what it's like for you!"

I know that they're trying to be understanding and kind, like they were when Jodie broke my rib, but their words fill me with complete rage. This is for the pure and irrational reason that I know for a fact that they're not finding any of the school work difficult.

I study hard every evening that I can, but like in the past, much of the content that I'm supposed to be revising I'm actually learning for the very first time. I spend most of my time when I'm supposed to be revising, searching the internet for explanatory videos made by crusty old examiners burbling about stuff which is most likely from the wrong exam board and/or from the old specification. My school life is like a tsunami, just waiting to wipe my name off the face of the earth, because if I don't pass my Maths GCSE and my art career never takes off, I am definitely one hundred percent gonna end up doing nothing with my life.

At some breaks and lunch times Madeline and Hafsa help me with Maths work, but they can't help me understand it. It appears that nobody can help me achieve at least a pass at GCSE Maths. Even attending Mr Plat's Maths clinic (which turns out to be a specialised class for me and Charlotte, another girl in the set who struggles) doesn't appear to make a huge difference.

* * *

The day before my first Maths mock paper I can hear my impending doom as it races nearer, waiting for the precise moment when it can pounce on me and strangle me until all of my artistic creativity is squeezed out of my body. I study late into the night and early into the next morning. It's half past five by the time I get into bed and half an hour later my alarm is screaming in my ears. I roll out of the safety of my warm comfortable duvet and go to have some breakfast. I am forced to plaster on under eye concealer to hide the dark shadows under my eyes. Even once I've stuck my wig on and styled it quite nicely, I still look like death warmed up.

My heart palpitates hard against my chest as I enter the exam hall, my crutches making a loud clicking sound which seems to echo around the walls.

"Use the nervous energy to help you get through the test," I remember Aunty Rose saying when she dropped me off this morning. "That's how I passed my nursing degree."

I follow her advice and check my flashcards just before the exam to make sure the knowledge is as secure as it can be. As I check over my notes on circle theorem they begin to make some form of sense. I am determined this time round to answer more than one question in the paper! I'm quite stunned to find that I know exactly what I'm doing for about ninety percent of all the test, so when Aunt Sophie comes to collect me at the end of the day I say with a smile,

"I think it might have gone okay actually."

"That's amazing," replies Aunt Sophie, beaming at these words."Your hard work is clearly starting to pay off isn't it?"

"I'm not too sure about that," I reply, pulling my seatbelt across my chest, "But I definitely think I got more than two percent like the last time I did a Maths assessment!"

That evening I am unable to read to Holly because I feel the need to revise for the mock exams tomorrow (English and German oral). I glance at the German vocab lists, which I've been making in my book for the last few weeks and I watch videos on all of the poems that we've been studying in English, working once again into the early hours of the morning to make sure that I can at least pass these assessments.

The remaining ten days of the mocks are like hell on earth. Sometimes there are up to three exams a day. Every day I have to tell Holly that I'll be unable to read to her that evening because I have to do my studying. Her sullen look is like a dagger through my heart every time. But every time I have to say,

"Once I've finished my exams, then I'll be back to reading to you every night. I promise."

I feel so sorry for Holly every time I say this, because I know that for a seven year old two weeks feels like forever.

My days in the examination period are extremely formulaic. They always follow the same pattern of food, work, then a few hours of sleep before I have to start another day of food, revision and zero fun whatsoever. I can't even have a laugh with Hafsa and Madeline at the break and lunchtimes because we're desperately revising on one of the picnic tables in the year ten playground, our work books spread out in front of us. We might test each other on some concepts sometimes but mostly it's just silent revision. After the exams we're going to have to let off steam big time!

Chapter 50

A week later the exams are finally over (relief), but I have an appointment with a doctor to check up on what's left of my left leg (stress).

"I'm sure the doctor will think you've done great," reassures Aunt Sophie just before we set off for the hospital.

"Yeah, I guess," I mumble. What do people mean when they say that I've done really well? Because I'll never be the same as I was almost a year ago now.

We wait in the crowded waiting room. There are children and adults with a whole range of limbs missing, however no one has skin that looks like mine does. We're waiting for nearly an hour to be seen. Every time a nurse comes out of one of the consultation rooms I'm wondering if it'll be my name that's called. While I'm waiting I'm actually able to complete most of the work which I'm missing today. I can't believe we're already doing classwork again when the exams are only just finished. *Do these teachers never give up!*

I seem to be becoming quite efficient at working independently on the subjects I struggle with. If there's one good thing that's come out of the accident, if that's even possible, it's that I now work far harder on my school work than I did last year.

"You look very well," says the doctor. Predictable.

"Thank you," I say.

"No really," she continues. "I never thought you'd look quite this well after I'd operated on you." I can feel myself blushing. Pearl was the one who would have blushed before. No way would it be me.

The doctor examines my scar, which is now just a ring of pale pigment surrounding the bottom of my stump.

"I'm very pleased," she announces, taking off her latex gloves and placing them in the bin.

"I've got a question for you," says the doctor a couple of minutes later, "Would you potentially be interested in us fitting you with a prosthetic for your left leg?"

"Prosthetic?" I echo back, not really understanding what this means.

"Essentially we make you a fake leg so that you can walk again."

Something sings inside me, like a whale-song deep beneath the waves.

"Yes," I smile, "I would *definitely* be interested in getting one of those."

I'm sent to another part of the clinic to have a cast made of my right-good-leg and what's left of my left leg for the prosthetic limb to be fitted. Giddy excitement fills my body.

"Will it look like a normal leg?" I ask, as the prosthetics clinician wraps a tape measure around my right thigh.

"No, I'm afraid that it won't look like the other leg but it'll enable you to do so much more than you can already do. We can offer you a selection of different types, like one for swimming and a different one for walking for example," he adds.

I think about the cool tranquil feeling of a swimming pool and imagine the relaxing splish-splash of my arms. Before today I didn't think that I'd be able to go on long walks ever again. That night as I lie in bed I'm filled with excited joy at the prospect of a new leg. It might stop some of the pitying looks at school. I'll be able to wear full length school trousers. I mean: sure it's not the skirt I was wearing last year, but it's progress.

I toss and turn in bed for a long time before I can fall asleep. It's like for the first time in a year I'm not trapped in the cage belonging to despair but instead welcomed into the home of happiness. It feels so refreshing to be kept awake not by fear, grief and anguish. Instead I'm kept awake by a light, pleasant, airy, tingly feeling and a silky smooth sense of security. I think I hear my sister's voice:

Things have been bad in the last year but maybe things will continue to get better and better.

Chapter 51

The next two weeks, while I'm waiting for my prosthetic leg to be made seem to drag by at a snail's pace. Maybe a dead snail actually!

"I can't believe that in ten days I'll have two legs again!" I exclaim excitedly to Hafsa and Madeline the day after saying,

"I can't believe that in eleven days I'll have two legs again!"

"It *is* very exciting," admits Hafsa, indulgently.

"We're so excited for you!" adds Madeline brightly.

"I've had an amazing idea," says Hafsa. "Once you get your prosthetic we'll do a photo shoot with you and your new leg? What do you think?"

"It's a great idea!" I say. My two friends always seem to come up with the very best concepts.

＊＊＊

"Are you getting a new leg?" asks Holly innocently, while eating a chocolate biscuit.

"Basically," I say, "Although it's not a real leg."

"Of course not," says Holly, "That would be silly."

"Yes," I say nodding. "That would be very silly," giving her a big hug.

＊＊＊

Finally the day arrives. I can hardly keep still as Aunt Sophie drives us to the hospital. Fortunately we don't have too long to wait this time.

"Here it is," says the clinician passing me a box. "This is your new walking leg. And this," she passes me another box, "is the leg for swimming again."

She takes the walking leg out of the box. She wasn't wrong when she said that it wouldn't look like a real leg. It's clear that it's been made in a factory. However it is my only hope of being able to walk again.

"It'll feel like a very big new shoe," the clinician explains. "Today is about checking the fit. Then we'll send you to the physio for a referral to Walking School. I believe you already know Bella, is that right?"

It sounds like it's not going to be as simple as putting on the prosthetic and running out of the door. At first I feel a bit flat. But then I remember it was Bella who got me out of my bed after my accident and is the reason that I'm able to hop around school all day. Everything takes time, especially the good things.

When the leg goes on for the first time it feels uncomfortable and alien. *Can I ever get used to it?*

"The fitting is perfect," says the clinician.

"How does it feel?" says Aunty Sophie.

"It feels weird," I reply, smiling uncertainly. "But it feels great too"

And it does feel amazing. I never thought that it would be possible for me to walk ever again without crutches, even if I do have to go to another school on top of the one that I'm doing already!

Aunt Sophie and Bella start going through the diary to put dates in for me to attend the walking classes.

"You'll need to go to Phylis House for the therapy" says Bella. "They'll be teaching you how to balance properly and walk in the right way so that you don't cause muscle injury. And you need to be patient. I don't mind you trying out the leg at home a little each day but don't overdo it. It's more about just getting used to the feeling of it at this early stage.

I'm beaming as we leave the hospital.

"I love it," says Holly encouragingly, pointing at my leg after I get home and have a go at putting it on myself. She is so impossibly mature for a child of seven years. She's always been amazingly grown up for her age but ever since I've lived here she's become one hundred times more adult. With that kind of demeanor I can really see her realising her dream of becoming a doctor one day.

"*It feels so cool,*" I write in the group chat to Madeline and Hafsa later.

"*So glad!*" replies Hafsa within like ten seconds.

"*Does that mean you'll be walking around school tomorrow?*" asks Madeline.

"*Not quite yet. I need to do some therapy for a few weeks first,*" I reply "*It's a start tho!*"

Later that evening I paint a picture of what it feels like to have my freedom given back to me. I paint myself, with two legs, walking away from an iron cage, with a huge smile on my face. The sky behind me is rainy and the sky in the direction I'm walking is sunny and clear. I do really think that my life may have had its hardship for the rest of time. The scars of losing Mum, Dad and Pearl, although still there, are beginning to heal. As I paint I wonder if I'll hear back from the art competition which I entered. I'm pretty sure that they'd have replied to me by now if I'd gotten anywhere in it. I guess I should wait maybe a month more before I make that judgement. To be fair the Tate Modern is a very famous art gallery and they probably had loads of interest from all over the globe. I'm not giving up hope yet.

As I lie in bed that night I think about the better life that must be heading my way, whether I win the competition or not. I know that even if I don't win, life can still be good because I'm surrounded by my friends and family who I love and who love me. I hear Pearl's soft voice saying,

"I'm so proud of you, Ocean. You've achieved so much lately. I'd never have been as brave as you've been."

"Yes you would," I whisper into the semi dark summer night, "You were the strongest person I ever knew, or know." I hear her laugh in the silky soft way that she always did.

"No way, you know that I was terrified of the dark until the age of twelve. You used to get really irritated with me when I'd have my nightlight on."

"That's true," I admit, "But I'm sorry, I was such a bitch to you when you were here sometimes. I need you to know how much I love you and value you as a sister, okay?"

I then hear her voice getting more and more quiet as if she's drifting away from me like a boat leaving a harbour as she says,

"Goodbye Oceay."

"Bye," I reply, "I'll never forget you."

"Me neither," she says and then there's silence and I'm pretty sure that this is the last time I'll hear her voice.

Chapter 52

I wake up on that morning, the morning of the first anniversary since the accident. I don't want to get out of bed for two reasons.

It's the holidays so why should I?

The other reason is I know that the day will be filled with flashbacks, even more perhaps than I normally have.

My bed feels like a safe haven. No matter where Holly and Jack want to go today there's no way I'm getting in a car. I don't suppose I'll ever get into a car on this day ever again.

"Today is all about you," says Aunty Rose. "What do you want to do? What would they have liked to do? What would Pearl have wanted to do?"

I think to myself for a second and then I say,

"I know exactly what she would have liked to do."

That afternoon we're walking through the park and we climb the hill in the middle. As always, it's green and beautiful. I know that she would have loved it here. Aunt Sophie carries a picnic basket, Jack and Holly run ahead. There's a soft summer breeze, just like there was a year ago today. And yes, I'm walking. It's still not perfect but Walking School was amazing and I know that by the start of term I'll be there.

We have an amazing day. I reflect on the family I've lost but how another section of the same family has taken me under their wing. We share memories of the family who are no longer here, both in a mental and physical sense. I find photos which were uploaded onto our Google Drive on my phone. I look over pictures of our family, frozen in a moment of silence. It's a picture of us at the beach, the year before the crash. Pearl and I are holding giant Mr Whippy ice creams. We both have white dairy cream around our mouths. Mum and Dad are forcing smiles. No one else could tell this by the way the photo looks, but I know what was going on. They'd been arguing just a few minutes previously about the fact that Mum seemed to never be around. I'll always love them of course but I wonder if they'd have argued as much if they'd known that an argument at the wrong moment would have ended in such a tragedy.

Aunty Rose raises a glass of lemonade, (I wish it was vodka.) She then says cheerily,

"To Ocean, Pearl, Max and Milly."

"To Ocean, Pearl, Max and Milly," says everyone else, raising their plastic cups and sipping at the same time.

We arrive back home later that evening. The house feels cool and refreshing after a day out in the sun. Aunty Rose kept plastering me in sun cream as if I was a child.

"We can't have those scars getting burned can we?" she insisted, rubbing factor fifty all over my face. I pretended to be cross but I wasn't really. My two Aunties clearly care about me so much and that feels like a big hug from the inside. We slump on the sofa gulping glass after glass of orange squash before we're even ready to have showers to wash off the perspiration from the hot summer's day.

The water in the shower feels cool and refreshing against my skin. I sing as I lather the soap on my hands and wash myself. It feels like I sing all the happy songs I know, one after another, sometimes changing tune mid verse. I get changed into a pair of denim shorts, like the shorts I wore a year ago today. I put some mascara and eyeliner on, making my eyes stand out. I put my wig back on and comb it out in front of the mirror. I smile at my straight white teeth and plump pink lips, which I've put a load of lippy on. I then go into the living room and collapse on the sofa again. Making yourself look nice is a real effort! I flip through the channels on the TV.

Aunty Rose comes in with a broad smile on her face.

"Ocean, there's a letter here for you."

She passes me the white envelope. It has Tate Modern printed on the thick white paper. I slowly open it, being careful not to rip whatever's inside. The paper feels smooth below my fingers.

"I'm surprised," I say, "I didn't think I'd hear anything back from them."

"So…?" asks Aunt Sophie, as I pull out the letter.

But no reply is needed, because the broad grin on my face says everything.

Epilogue (12 years later)

My life is great. It's amazing how much my life has improved since the end of year ten.

Everyone now knows me as Ocean Rodrigo, 'the youngest ever person to win the competition put on by the Tate Modern'. It feels so incredible to be known about by so many art lovers and I feel incredibly fortunate. I frequently receive emails from people from all over the world telling me how much they love my work and what an inspiration I am and some tell me that they have my pieces proudly displayed on their walls. I love the fact that people feel empowered to get through the challenges in their lives whenever they see my art work and hear about the struggles that I've faced. I really hope that my pieces of work make a difference. I want it to nourish people's minds and souls. I'm glad that I make people feel happy because I think that's what life should be about: helping people to get through the times in their life where they feel like the sun will never come out again. People need to realise that their lives can become better, once they've got through the hardships.

I'm still extremely close to my extended family. I talk to Jack and Holly almost everyday. I am so proud of both of them. Holly is in her first year of training and hopes to become an A&E doctor, working in the trauma team.

"You've inspired me," she said when she received her A level results and got into Cardiff Medical school, "Because you've shown me that if someone gets the right kind of care and support, they can live a normal and enriched life."

Jack has now finished his first year of A levels and he hopes to become an environmental scientist.

"We all have to do our bit to keep the world safe for future generations," he's explained to me on more than one occasion. "I don't want to look back and think I didn't do enough for our planet."

It's strange to think that my baby cousins are now adults pursuing their dreams and ambitions. My baby cousins, who I read to and played with, are now older than I was when I went to live with them! And my two wonderful Aunties who gave me so much in the lowest point of my life and to whom I will always be eternally grateful, they helped me see, with the help of Jade, that life is still worth living even when it hasn't gone the way you thought it would.

I go to visit Dad and Pearl's graves on any special days: mine and Pearl's birthday, Christmas, Easter and the anniversary of our accident. I am also now comforted in the knowledge that Mum is with Dad and Pearl. I'm glad because this way she doesn't have to suffer any more.

Visiting the graves is a tradition I started five years ago. I like to have a quiet moment when I can just sit and reflect and speak to their engraved stones. I can never hold back the tears when I talk to the empty space, but that's okay because I know that sometimes everyone should allow themselves a moment, just a small amount of time to let the emotions they've been holding in so bravely be released like a caged bird. I tell them about my art work, films I've watched since the last visit and my daughter.

My beautiful, angelic amazing daughter. She's so smart, funny and kind, despite only being three years old. Whenever I'm not painting, I'm singing with her or playing hide and seek with her or taking her to her baby ballet classes. When she dances around in her baby pink leotard and skirt and soft white ballet pumps, I feel pride bursting from my chest.

She's my little phenomenon and that's why I called her Pearl.

She's mine, and that makes her Ocean's Pearl.

Acknowledgements

Huge thanks to Rachel Walsh for her fantastic cover artwork. Thanks also to Tom Poole for his help with some of the medical specifics after the accident. Emily Jellett was a brilliant final proof reader and my family are always encouraging and ready to pick me up when I feel like throwing the whole book away and starting again. I guess anyone who writes knows that feeling!

About the author

Rowan Todd was born and grew up in Guildford in the United Kingdom. Diagnosed with a brain tumor caused by Neurofibromatosis Type 1 when she was three, she underwent several years of chemotherapy before she was ten. As a consequence she is now a braille user and writes her work on an electronic braille machine. Talking books and music were her closest companions during treatment and she hopes to continue with her writing long into the future. She is a passionate activist for issues around the Climate Crisis and has been an active supporter of the Youth Strikes movement.

Lightning Source UK Ltd.
Milton Keynes UK
UKHW011444161221
395754UK00003B/194